A Bossed Up Holiday

New Year, New Man

By. Tyanna

A Bossed up Holiday

*****Synopsis*****

Tyrell already had his hands full with the death of his father and his mother's break down. With the holidays near, his focus is now primarily on his franchise. While investigating his store's books, he comes across the alluring Sarai. After little time together, he already feels the need to love and protect her. The only problem is she has secrets that could change everything.

Sarai was doing everything she could to hold her and her kids' world together this holiday season! After losing the love of her life, being betrayed by those close to her and being mistreated at work, her trust is limited. Needless to say, looking for love was not on her to-do list, but meeting Tyrell may change all of that!

Chapter 1

Sarai

I was standing at my register fiddling with my long blonde box braids wondering when I was goin' to get my break. I had been at work since 7a.m, and it was now 1p.m. I should have been gotten a break being as though I've been here since seven, but of course Sharp was on his bullshit today. Bringing me out of my thoughts, I heard my name being called on the loud speaker. That meant that Mr. Sharp wanted me to come to his office. I was hoping he only wanted me to go over my schedule for next week. I've been picking up so much overtime trying to get up money to give my kids a big Christmas. I asked Terry, my co-worker, to take over my register while I went to see what Mr. Sharp wanted. I headed to the back of the store, and when I made it to his office, I knocked on the door.

"Come in, Sarai, and lock the door behind you." Once he said lock the door, I knew it was going to be some shit. I couldn't stand his fat, sloppy ass; I wish he would just die.

"What is it Mr. Sharp?" He looked at me with a grin on is fat ugly White face.

"I wanted to know what days you want for next week." I looked at him like he was crazy because he could have just made a schedule up and gave it to me.

"You already know what schedule I've been doing, Mr. Sharp; just leave it the same." I already have a baby sitter for the schedule he's been giving me so I hope he's not trying to be an asshole.

"Well, it was a problem with some of those shifts, and I had to give some of those days to the other girls." I knew he had some bullshit up his sleeve before I came in here.

"I can keep the schedule the same for you. Under one condition." He said with that dumb ass smirk on his face. I swear I was sick of this shit, but anything for my babies. Ever since Mr. Sharp caught me stealing out the safe he's been blackmailing me. I had a hard time finding this job, so I was doing anything to keep it. I don't have any education so it's hard finding a job.

"Ok Mr. Sharp, what do you want me to do?" He slid his chair back from behind the desk and already had his white little pencil dick out. I almost threw up in my mouth just thinking about him making me suck that little shit.

"Get over here and suck my cock!" I was crying the whole time I was walking over to him. I knew that if I didn't do as I was told I could be fired and arrested; I couldn't do that to my babies. I proceeded to do as I was told, and nothing was said; all that was heard was slurping and sucking. As soon as I swallowed his little pecker this asshole had the nerve to grab a handful of my braids. I felt him speeding up the pace, so I knew he was near his peak. He would always try to nut in my mouth, but I would hurry up and move out of his way. Thanking God that he didn't have a tight grip on my hair, I was able to hurry and move out of the way.

"Ahhhhhhhhhhh!" Why you move you little bitch. Now, you lost one of those days you were getting back?" I didn't say shit to him. I just got up and walked to the bathroom to get myself together, so I could head back out to finish my break.

"Thanks again, Sarai. I appreciate what you do for me; you're a great worker." I didn't respond. I just walked out and was going to sit in my car for a minute. I knew I was going to cry the whole time I sat in my car. I needed to get all my crying out, so I could get back to work.

My name is Sarai Moore and I'm a 28-year-old cashier at Macy's that's living in hell right now. Everything was cool in my life until my kids' dad was gunned down a year ago. Trey made sure me and the kids were taken care of; he gave us the world. Where I messed up at was not doing for myself and saving money. Trey did it all; I didn't have to work. I knew that street money wasn't guaranteed so I should have had a backup plan. I knew about the money in Trey's safes but his right hand came and robbed all of them. I knew about the life insurance policy he had, but his Momma was the beneficiary and she didn't give me a dime to help with the kids. Trey didn't have a living will so nothing was in writing. It seems like when Trey died I lost all the friends I had; his family stopped fucking with me. Terry tapping on my window brought me out of my thoughts.

"Girl, your brake is almost over. I knew you were out here, so I came to tell you. I didn't want you to come in late. You know fat ass Sharp be acting up." I hurried up and hopped out my car, so I could run back in. Lord knows I didn't want to deal with Sharp's ass no more today.

"Thank you, Terry." I beamed while getting myself together before I excited the car. Terry and I have gotten close lately. She doesn't know anything about Sharp blackmailing me and I wanted to keep it that way. I made it back to my register just in time. Casey, my supervisor, ran over to tell me to make sure I had my name tag on, and my area was clean. The store owner was coming in to do his rounds. Once a month, he would come out to check out the store. I'm usually off when he comes, but I heard he was young, with brown skin, and fine as hell. When I heard he was only 30 years old I couldn't believe someone so young owned the store. I started looking in the register to see if my hair was straight and to make sure my eyes weren't puffy. Then I thought to myself why am I tripping; this man ain't checking for somebody like me. Don't get me wrong, I was pretty with light brown skin, and long pretty hair that I inherited from my mama. I had a small nose piercing that I thought was cute. I would wear very little make-up to work, but I was definitely a fan of a good face beat from time to time. I was slim but had a nice set of boobs and a little round bootie. I just dressed average though 'cause money was tight. I guess I just figured that I was beneath him. He was a store owner and I was one of his employees. That happened to live in the hood. Not to mention I got this job through one of those welfare programs.

Tyrell

It was now the middle of November and it was finally starting to get cold out, but that didn't stop me from taking my morning run. When my run was finished, I always stopped to get coffee. I was kind of getting sick of the same old routine every day, but that's what happens when you're not in a relationship, and don't have any kids. I was in this big ass house alone, and definitely growing tired of it. I used to love the holidays when my father was living; it would always be me, him, and my mama. My dad had been gone for a year now and shit just hasn't been the same. When he died, my mama lost it and had to be committed to a mental institution. I make sure I go visit her as much as my schedule allows me to.

 I miss the way my family used to be. I guess if I had a family of my own, I wouldn't feel so bad. The way my work hours are set up I never have time to date. When I do meet chicks, they only sticking around to see what my pockets are hitting for. I need somebody I can talk to, be friends with, and love all at the same time. But being Tyrell McKnight, the owner of all the Macy's Department Stores in the New Jersey area made it hard to settle down. I inherited my franchise from my pops. He worked his ass off to get where he was in the business when he passed. He started out as a store manager years ago. I didn't believe his story when he used to tell me about it when I was younger. My mom would always say this job would be the death of my dad. My mama wanted more kids, but my dad let the job take over his life.

 Right now, I don't have a family so that's why I stay stuck in my work. I always tell myself that when I get a family of my own, I would cut down this work load and let the people under me handle it. I didn't have a lot of friends. As a matter of fact, I had one best friend that I grew up with. I did have a couple of colleagues that I went out to the strip club with sometimes. I needed to get up and get myself together. I was doing a pop up at my Cherry Hill location. I wanted to know who this one particular lady was that was getting all these hours and I also wanted to check the store out. I've been hearing some shit about this Sharp person. I've wanted to fire him since I took over, but my mom always told me to leave him alone; he was one of my father's loyal workers. So, I left him alone but shit's starting to not add up with the sales for this particular store and I needed to get to the bottom of it.

I got up from my table and headed to take my shower. I didn't want to do the suit thing today so I was going to pop up on they asses with some regular shit on. I decided on a pair of boot cut Polo Jeans, and a hunter green Polo shirt with a gold horse on it, and a pair of wheat Tim's. I walked in my bathroom, turned the water on and put it to the temperature I liked before I hopped in. I put my dreads up in a bun on top of my head. I wasn't trying to get them all wet up. After making sure my hair was straight, I took my glasses off, placed them on the sink, then jumped in the shower. I washed my body a couple of times then rinsed a couple of times, and let the water run down my body once more before I hopped out. Once I made my way into my bedroom, I hurried and put some lotion and deodorant on before I got dressed. Exactly a half hour later, I was now ready to head out. I usually call a couple of days before to let the store manager know when I'm coming, but not today. I was about to call right now. I pulled out my iPhone X and dialed the number to the Cherry Hill branch.

"Hello, Macy's in Cherry Hill. Tara speaking; how may I direct your call?"

"Hello, can I speak to the general manager please?" I looked down at my watch to see how long it took for him to get on the phone. Ten minutes had gone by, and I was still waiting on somebody to get on the phone; if I was a customer I would have hung up by now.

"Hello, this is Joe Sharp speaking! How may I direct your call?"

"Hello Sharp, this is McKnight. I'm the store owner of this branch and I just wanted to inform you that I'm on my way there for my monthly visit." I could tell he was in shock and wasn't ready; he hesitated before he responded.

"Ummmmm ok, sir. I'll see you when you arrive." I laughed as soon as I disconnected the call. I thought to myself that I hope I don't have to fire anyone; it's too close to the holidays. I grabbed my briefcase and my black pea coat and headed out the door. I hit the alarm on my 2018 Benz truck and hopped in. I needed my motivation music so I programmed my phone to the Bluetooth in the car. I started my truck up and pulled off. I wasn't far away, so I knew I would get there in no time.

I made it to the store in about 20 minutes. I hopped out my truck and headed in the building. Everything seemed to be running smoothly in the front of the store; all registers were open, and the store was packed because the holidays were approaching. I headed to the back of the store to get up with the general manager; nobody knew who I was, and I liked it that way. I got to the door that said General Manager and knocked on the door. I met Sharp's fat nasty looking ass so he knew who I was already. He opened the door and moved to the side to let me in. I hated coming in his office. It always had a funny smell.

"Hey Mr. McKnight, what brings you this way today?" He already knew I was here for my monthly tour of the building and to go over the books.

"You know why I'm here, Sharp, so open up your computer." I needed to see payroll, and the numbers we were bringing in at the end of the day.

"Ok sir, you can sit behind my desk." I was ok standing; it smelled too bad in here for me to sit down anywhere; it had a sweaty and musty type of odor.

"I'm good, Sharp. I'll stand, but I'm going to need you to get some air freshener or something in here." The way he looked at me I knew he didn't like what I just said to him, but I didn't give a fuck. He logged in his computer and went to payroll. I seen a couple of chicks that were in the system as part time, but their pay check showed they were getting full-time hours and overtime.

"Who are these two and why do they have so many hours if they're part time employees?" Sharp sat there for a minute before he answered me like he was trying to get his story straight.

"Well, Mr. McKnight, Sarai is one of the best workers you have in this building, and Terry was having a hard time and needed extra hours."

"Why haven't you moved Sarai up if she's such a great worker?" If she's such a great worker like he says she should have been moved up to at least a shift supervisor.

"I don't know, sir, but I'll get right on it." I wanted to meet this Ms. Sarai before I left this building. I looked over a couple more things in the computer with the employees and made a couple more changes then I went on my tour. I figured I would be in this store for a while today to get shit in order.

Chapter 2

Terry

I hurried and ran out to Sarai's car to let her know the store owner was coming in. I saw her coming from the back of the store looking like she had just been crying. I laughed at her stupid ass. Sharp had her dumb ass wrapped around his finger. I hated that Sharp showed her more attention than me. I didn't know why I sucked his dick and fucked him on the regular. I came up with a plan for me and him to rob the store safes, and if they start catching on we were going to blame it on Sarai. I know y'all wondering why I'm setting up my friend but fuck her high sidity ass. Sarai thanks she's all that; she gets all the hours around here, and Sharp always talks about Sarai this, Sarai that, but man fuck her. I get heated just thinking about it. I've been here for way longer than her and she gets all the hours and she works in every department. They always keep my ass on clean up or the register only if the store is packed. I know it sounds like I'm jealous, but so what; maybe I am.

Sarai thought nobody knew about her sucking Sharp's little ass dick. I knew all about it from the day he caught her stealing out the safe up until her sucking his little dick an hour ago; nothing goes past me that has to do with Sharp. I know y'all probably have your noses turned up thinking about me fucking with Sharp, but hey, my bills stay paid and I have his money and my own.

I was headed to the back to go clean the bathrooms and I saw this fine ass brown skin nigga headed to the back of the store. He was laced in all Polo and a pair of crisp wheat Tim's; all I smelled was his Polo Double Black tickling the insides of my nostrils. I watched this man the whole time he headed to the back until he was out of my view. I swear daddy had it going on. I was assuming he was headed to see Sharp. I couldn't wait to find out the scoop who he was.

 Sharp's dumb fat ass tells me everything I want to know as long as I feed and fuck him. I can get anything I want. I continued to clean the bathrooms then I was assigned to customer service the rest of my shift. I had an easy workload every day thanks to Sharp since I couldn't be a manager or supervisor. I made sure he kept my workload light. I finished the bathrooms and headed up front and when I made it to customer service I noticed I was working with Ms. Haddy. I couldn't stand her old ass; she made sure my ass was working while I was up here. She was the oldest worker in the store. I couldn't wait to talk to Sharp's ass and curse him out for scheduling me with her. I swear every department store has an old employee that been in the building since it was built from the ground and that was Ms. Haddy's irking ass.

"Hey Terry, how are you baby?" Ms. Haddy asked while smiling at me. I couldn't wait to check Sharp for this bullshit.

"Hey Ms. Haddy, I'm good." I kept it short and simple with her and went over to my register. Ms. Haddy must have sensed my attitude because she spoke on it.

"Listen here, little girl. I'm not going to tolerate your attitude today, and I don't care what type of relationship you and Sharp got going on." I looked at Ms. Haddy like she lost her fucking mind talking to me like she doesn't have it all. I walked over to her and got close enough to be in her ear but changed my mind when I saw Sharp walk up with Mr. Sexy I seen in the back.

"Hello, ladies this is Mr. McKnight, the store owner," Sharp said as he walked over to introduce us all to this fine ass store owner. I couldn't believe this was the store owner; he was a young ass boss that I wouldn't mind getting to know. I could tell the way Sharp was looking at me lusting over the store owner that he was getting heated, but I didn't give a damn.

"Hello, Mr. McKnight, nice to meet you. I'm Terry Clark," I spoke to the store owner while licking my lips. I hope I wasn't looking too thirsty. He said hello, but that shit was dry as hell like he didn't want to speak. He was so caught up into seeing Ms. Haddy he didn't give a damn about my hello. Ms. Haddy ran from behind the register and gave him a big hug and kiss.

"Is that you, Tye; how are you baby; you look just like your daddy." Mr. McKnight smiled and hugged her back.

"Hey Ms. Haddy, how are you. I haven't seen you in such a long time." They were bussing it up like they were relatives, so I went back to my work. I felt like I got dissed for an old ass lady. He and Ms. Haddy were still talking when Sarai walked up to get change. It's like the world stood still the way they were staring at each other. Sharp cleared his throat to get their attention before he introduced Sarai.

"Mr. McKnight, this is Sarai, the one I told you about." Sarai looked up at him and smiled, and he smiled back and shook her hand.

"Well, hello Ms. Sarai. I heard so much about you in such a little time, and I would like to talk to you about a new position before I leave here today." I was furious because whatever he heard had to come from Sharp fat ass, and the way Mr. McKnight held Sarai's hand while he talked to her had my blood boiling. This nigga act like my hand was contagious but holding her shit like she's the Queen of Sheba.

Mr. Sharp

I was sitting behind my desk still coming off my high from the good dick sucking that Sarai just gave me. I think I'm in love with Sarai, but I knew she would never have me so I used her the best way I knew how. I know it's not right but nobody that looks as good as she wants a fat ass White man with no real money. I have to do something with Terry's ass; she was costing me too much money, and I was putting my job in jeopardy. I had her thinking she was running shit, but that bitch wasn't running shit around here. She had it in her mind we were robbing the safes and going to blame Sarai for it, but I had some shit up my sleeve. I was going to put all the blame on her.

When I got the phone call that McKnight was popping up it shocked the hell out of me. I made sure I called a quick meeting to inform everybody to be on their shit because the owner was coming. I knew I wasn't running this store the way it should be run, but I thought I was doing the best I could. I was hoping that he didn't catch on to the numbers not matching up like they are supposed to. I was sitting at my desk when I heard a knock at my door. I opened it and in walked Tyrell McKnight.

I didn't like his ass just like I couldn't stand his daddy. After he told me to get some air freshener in here I knew I was going to be pissed for the rest of the day. He looked through my computer and asked a couple of questions, and then he told me to follow him. So, I knew we were going on a tour. We stopped and checked all the bathrooms and the staff lounge. Then we made our way up to customer service.

Terry's hoe ass was just lusting over him while he talked to Ms. Haddy. The shit pissed me off since she always tells me how she feels about me. After he was done hugging and talking to Ms. Haddy, Sarai walked up, and it was like the world stopped when the two looked at each other. I was already mad that he wanted to give her a raise and up her position. This would mean I couldn't blackmail her ass anymore.

"Hello Mr. McKnight, it's nice to meet you. My shift will be over in another hour. I have to rush out of here to get my kids from the babysitter on time. Is it possible we can talk before the shift ends?" Sarai asked in a low tone with her head down twiddling with her fingers.

"Yes…that can happen. Sharp, put somebody on the register, and Sarai go close out and meet me back over here. I wanna finish up the tour with you. I'm sure you know what goes on around here. Sharp, I'll call you to the office when I'm done with the rest of the tour."

"Ok, sir… no problem. Terry, you can go cover the register that Sarai was on. Ms. Haddy, you can handle over here alone. If it gets to be too much just call my office and I'll come out here with you." Terry got an attitude when I told her to cover the register, but I didn't care; she would be just fine. What I didn't like was the way McKnight was looking at Sarai.

After I made all the switches, I headed back to my office to clean up and place some air fresheners inside. When I was done, I sat at my desk and went through some things on my computer in case McKnight wanted to look into my work a little more when he came back. A knock at my door brought my eyes away from my computer. I got up and opened it.

"Hey hunny, what are you doing here?" I asked my wife while moving to the side, so she could walk in.

"I've been calling you all day Joe."

"Cindy, I've been busy all day. Today, the store owner is in the building doing his monthly inspection. I didn't have time to answer no phone calls. What do you want that you couldn't wait until I made it home?"

"I just wanted to make sure you made it to Joe Jr's Holiday play."

"I have so much work to do here, but I'll try to make it."

"You know what Joe. I don't know why I waisted my time coming all the way up here. All you wanna do is be at this damn store all the time. I know you doing more than working all the time, and if I ever find out who she is I'm coming for you and her Joe." Cindy yelled and stormed out.

When she left the office, I turned on the cameras to see exactly where Sarai and McKnight were at. The sight before me pissed me off; they were all laughing and enjoying their conversation. I hated that she looked so happy in his presence. I wish I could hear what they were

talking about, but I knew that wasn't possible. I wonder
what his plans for her were. I knew he was taking her on
the tour to see how much she knew. So, he could determine
exactly how high of a position she deserved.

Chapter Three

Sarai

My shift was over, but I still hadn't made it home. I was standing out in the cold crying 'cause my car wouldn't start. Erica, my neighbor that kept an eye on my kids, was pissed off. All she kept doing was calling back to back. Her man was coming over and he didn't do kids. So, while he was over, I had her kids and mine. I slammed the hood of the car shut and leaned on the door. *Lord why me? I swear I can never catch a break.* I cried to myself. I got some amazing news today, and I was extremely happy until this happened.

"Sarai are you ok?" A familiar voice said bringing me out of my zone. I tried wiping the tears from my eyes before I looked up at him.

"I'm ok Mr. McKnight." I lied knowing damn well I was far from ok.

"For starters, Sarai, it's after work hours and you've clocked out already. So, please call me Tyrell. I know you're not good 'cause I can tell you've been crying."

"All right, Tyrell, I guess you caught me. My car won't start, and I need to get my kids. The babysitter keeps calling, and I think I just messed up with her. So, I don't know what I'm going to do with my kids tomorrow, so I can work. I definitely can't afford to miss no days."

"I'll take you to get your kids, and make sure you all get home safe."

"Mr. Mc--- I mean Tyrell I can't ask you to do that."

"Come on Sarai… I won't take no for an answer. Leave ya car here, and I'll make sure it gets towed to your mechanic tomorrow."

"I don't have a mechanic. Besides, it's a month away from Christmas. I can't afford to get that car fixed right now." I sighed while grabbing my purse and phone out of my passenger seat.

When I headed over to Tyrell's truck he got out and opened the door for me. He didn't close the door until he made sure I was sitting in the front seat safely. When I looked up at him to thank him our eyes met once again just like they did earlier. I smiled when he winked and that broke our intense stare.

"So, where are we headed to?"

I thought about where I lived, and embarrassment came over me. I had dreams of getting out of the hood one day, but when Trey died all of those dreams went straight out of the window.

"I live in McGuire Gardens on Berwick Street."

"Ok…I know exactly where that is. I grew up in Pennsauken; my pops tried to keep me away from McGuire, but I always found my way back. My boy Cam grew up out here."

"Cameron Johnson?" I asked in shock.

"Yeah, that's him." Tyrell chuckled.

"How I know Cam, but I never met you?" I asked in shock.

"When I used to come over Ms. Candice didn't really let us out. If anything, she would take us out then back in the house we would go. So, it's a possibility the days I did make it out on the step you weren't out." Knowing that he was familiar where he was goin' and that he had a friend from my hood, I didn't feel embarrassed like I did a little while ago.

The ride to my house was quiet. I was so happy for the raise I had gotten, but I was scared my babysitter wasn't goin' to come through with me. When I noticed we were about to turn off the highway, I gave Tyrell the address for the babysitter's house.

"Tyrell I wanna thank you so much for giving me a ride. I really appreciate it."

"No thanks needed Sarai." He said right before getting out to open the door for me.

Once I got out, he stayed watching me. I guess to make sure I got in the house. The minute I walked in Erica was standing there with her hand on her hips.

"Sarai, I hope you know you owe me extra. You made me miss my damn date, and he rescheduled for tomorrow. So, I ain't gone be able to get them from school or watch them for you." I knew she was goin' to be on the bullshit. I didn't say anything 'cause I didn't feel like arguing with her. I hope she found someone to watch her own damn kids.

"Hey, mama…I was wondering when you were going to get here." My seven-year-old Sierra said. She was the oldest out of my three. Sage is five and Treyvon Jr. is three. It's like once Trey and I started we didn't stop. All I could do was shake my head. I wasn't ashamed of my babies and I didn't regret having them. I just wish I had myself more established. Instead of just living off of Trey's street money. Every day I wish I would have taken my ass to college or took up a trade or something. Being on welfare and living in the projects wasn't in the plans for me. I gathered all my babies and headed out of the house not paying Erica's ass any mind when she continued to talk about tomorrow. Just like she couldn't watch my kids I wouldn't be keeping hers.

When I made it outside, to my surprise, Tyrell was still sitting out there. I told the kids to stay on the step and I walked up to his car.

"What are you still doing here?"

"I was waiting on you. Your home is still a couple of blocks away and it's cold out. Come on; get the kids and put them in the car, so I can take you home."

I did as he said and walked back over to get the kids. After I got the kids all settled in the back seat. Tyrell jumped out of the car and opened the passenger seat door for me. I couldn't do shit but blush. Where the fuck did this man come from.

"Mama…who is this man?" Sierra's little-grown ass asked.

"Sierra, this is my boss, Mr. Tyrell."

"Hey…Mr. Tyrell, thanks for the ride; it's cold out there." I shook my head. While he laughed.

"You're welcome little lady." He beamed. Five minutes went by and he was pulling up in front of my house. I jumped out and helped the kids into the house. I told Sierra to watch them while I went back out to talk to Tyrell.

"I wanna thank you for all you did for me today. Good people are definitely hard to come by these days."

"I told you it wasn't a problem, and I'll tell Sharp that you won't be in for a couple of days. Get your babysitting situation and transportation together before you return." My lip dropped to the ground when he said that. It's no way I could take days off. I really can't afford it.

"Tyrell, I really can't afford to take any days off for the next couple of months. My rent just went up and I could barely afford to do anything for my kids for the holidays. Thanksgiving is coming up and so is Christmas. Plus, my car just broke down and I have to pay a babysitter. I have too much to do and I can't be taking days off." I didn't mean to just tell him all my business, but shit it was all the truth. I needed all my coins to make it.

Tyrell got out of the car and leaned on it while standing next to me. I felt so embarrassed once again after telling him my situation. I held my head down and fiddled with my fingers. I could feel him staring at me, but I refused to look up.

"I'm sure you have some type of time where you can take off with pay. If not, I'll make sure that you do. I know you feel like your back is against the wall and you never can catch a break. But baby girl ya time is coming real soon." He said while grabbing my chin and making me look up at him. While I was getting my words together, I looked deep into his eyes before choosing my choice of words.

"Why?" I asked just above a whisper.

Shit was starting to get straight suspect. Like, why was this nigga helping me like this? He didn't even know anything about me. As a matter of fact, he just met me today. So, what was his angle?

"I see you need the help, so why not help you. I know it seems weird since I just met you today, but don't be alarmed. I do what I do 'cause I want to. Plus, I can tell you go hard for your kids and I'm impressed by that. So, if I'm willing to help let me."

"What do you want in return? Niggas just don't help for the hell of it?"

"I don't want nothing in return baby girl."

"I'm sorry, Tyrell; that came out all wrong. I appreciate everything you're doing. I'm just not used to all of this. Maybe I can repay you by cooking you dinner or something like that."

"Oh, so you can throw down in the kitchen?"

"Yeah, my mama did teach me something when she wasn't high."

"Alright, well here's my phone; program your number in, and I'll shoot you a text, so you'll have my number. Remember, I'll have Sharp give you a couple of sick days or something, so you won't miss no pay."

"Ok, Tyrell…thanks so much for doing this for me. I'll text you tomorrow to let you know when I'll be able to get back to work. I have to figure out something with this damn car. Even if it's not fixed in a couple of days, I can always catch the bus to work."

"Don't stress ya self out about it today. Go ahead in the house with the kids and relax. Worry about all that other stuff tomorrow. It'll get handled somehow."

Everything he was saying was better said than done. I did need to relax to get my thoughts together. After I told him goodbye, I headed in the house, and the kids were sitting down watching cartoons. I walked to my room and fell right on my bed. Today had been a bit much and all I could do was cry. I was sick of crying though; I wish soon God would answer my prayers.

Tyrell

"So, how's mama doing?"

"She's doing really good. They said she's been acting normal with the meds. They even told me that I may be able to bring her out for the holidays. I'm so excited about that since I've spent the last couple of holidays at that place eating dinner with her. It would be such a blessing bringing her out."

"That's what's up. I'm glad to hear that."

"Yo, I came here to tell you about my visit to the Cherry Hill Branch. I swear I don't like that nigga Sharp. It's something suspect about his ass. So, I'ma start doing pop-ups more often. But I met this chick named Sarai. I wanted to know why her ass had been getting all this time. So, I go in and ask him, and he tells me she's one of the best workers he has. I'm like well, why hasn't she been put up to full-time or even a supervisor; shit, she is killing hours already. He is sitting there looking at me all clueless and shit. Speaking of Sarai, I meant to ask you do you remember her from when y'all were younger. She still lives out McGuire; her last name is Moore."

"Yeah…I know her. I haven't seen her in years. I heard her dude got shot up a couple of years ago. Leaving her with three babies. What about her?"

"That's the chick that works at the job. I don't know what it is about her, but when we first made eye contact, we got stuck. Next thing I know I'm making her full-time and upping her pay rate. Then on my way home she was still in the parking lot cause her car broke down. So, I ended up taking her to pick her kids up then dropping them off at home."

"Rai cool peoples, but is you ready to take on three kids bro. That's a lot of baggage."

"I don't know what I'm ready for, but all I know is I wanna help her. This shit is crazy; it's like the minute I looked into her pretty eyes all I wanted to do is be her peace. I could tell by the sadness in her eyes that she's goin' through some shit."

"Man…I'm not gone tell you what to do. But Rai is a different type of female from what you're used to. Not to mention she has never been with a guy like you. Baby girl use to drug dealers and shit like that."

"I mean I'm not a drug dealer, but I'm making boss moves like any slinger out here. I just do my shit the legal way. Its money coming in but just not the illegal way. Shit, you know I can get down if need be, so don't try to play me like that Cam."

"I'm not saying like that bro. I know you got it and you can get down. But will you be able to handle her ways? Not saying that she hood or anything, but she just a different breed from what you used too. That's all I'm saying."

"As long as she makes me feel good and we both comfortable, I don't care about her upbringing bro. I got plenty of money and I don't mind sharing it."

"You all talking like she money hungry or something Cam." Keonna came walking into the living room bringing us out of our conversation.

"Baby… that's not what I'm saying."

"Well, exactly what are you saying then. I was born and raised in the suburbs and you were brought up in the hood. But that doesn't change how I feel about you or how you treated me."

"I guess you're right. With ya nosey ass. You all the way in the kitchen ear hustling."

"So, what. I'm just trying to give Tye a woman's point of view. I say go for whatever your heart is telling you to do Tye. You're single; it doesn't hurt to try it out. It's new and it might turn out to be right. Don't listen to Cam; he doesn't know what he is talking about." She kissed Cam on the cheek and walked off.

We both chuckled and watched her walk back into the kitchen. Cam and Keonna had been married for a year now, and they were getting ready for their first child which was due in about six months. I get Cam was looking out for me, but shit he had his family already, and I was on a search for mine. I didn't know I was goin' to come out of my house and find someone I was interested in; this must have been destined to happen. Keonna was cooking dinner, so I decided to stay a little longer, so I could buss a grub. Then I made my way home to shower and just chill.

The minute I made it home, I went into the kitchen, grabbed me a water, and made my way upstairs to shower. An hour went by and I was now sitting at my desk on my computer checking on a couple of other stores. I knew November and December were the biggest months of the year for retail. They also were the months I did the most work. I know y'all think the store owners don't be doing much, but these particular months I did a lot of hands-on to make sure the holiday season was running correctly. It was the middle of November and all Christmas decorations were up. I had made sure night shift in every store did that the first week of November. The thought of the holidays made Sarai come to mind, and I had forgotten to text her, so she would have my number.

Me: Hey this is Tyrell. Sorry, I'm late texting you.

Sarai: You good… I just got finished bathing and putting the kids to bed.

Me: Ok, well I'ma let you go. I know you have to be up early with the kids in the morning.

Sarai: Alright, and thanks again for today Tyrell.

Me: No thanks needed. Good night sweetheart!

After I was finished texting her, I remembered to send Sharp an email letting him know that he needed to find coverage for her and she would be taking some time off. Then I called my boy Ted to tow her car to my mechanic. If I didn't think she would freak out I probably would have bought her a new one, but I didn't wanna seem too pressed.

Once I was finished all the business I had to attend to, I took my tired ass to bed with thoughts of Sarai on my mind.

Chapter Four

Mr. Sharp

I woke up to McKnight's email and got an instant attitude. I didn't have anybody to cover for her but Terry and I knew she was goin' to have an attitude when I called her in.

"What's wrong with you Joe?" Cindy asked.

"Nothing…just know I'ma have a long day at work."

"I don't understand why you don't own one of those stores yet. You've been working for the McKnight's for so many years he should have given you a damn store."

"Cindy…don't start this morning."

"I'm just saying, you know all the retail stuff. If you were bringing in good money, maybe you could own a store of your own. You've been there all these years and you still making this little bit of money. I wish you go elsewhere. Maybe they will start you off with what you deserve."

Cindy was a pain in my ass. I could have been left the McKnight's, but I had it good. I didn't want the big responsibility of owning my own store, so that's why I stayed where I was. Money was coming in fine. It just wasn't what Cindy wanted being as though she stayed her lazy ass home. Other than doing what the fuck I wanted, I was able to mess with all these simple ass young girls from the Welfare program.

"Cindy…I just said don't start this morning. I'm not in the mood."

"Since you're not in the mood, make your own damn breakfast."

After fussing with Cindy for a little while longer, I decided to just leave out and stop at Wawa to get me a cup of coffee and a bagel. As soon as I got into the car, I called Terry to let her know she had to come in to cover for Sarai's shift. Pulling out my phone, I decided to hook the call up to my car, so I could talk as I pulled off.

"Hello…what do you want this early Joe? I'm tired and don't feel like talking."

"You have to work today. Sarai won't be back for a couple of days, and I'ma need you to cover her shifts for a couple of days. Before you start all the yelling and smart talk, this is per Mr. McKnight. If you don't wanna work the hours, I'll give him your number and have him call you himself. I'll see you when I get to the job." I said while hanging up. I knew she was about to go off, and tonight just wasn't my day. I swear these women weren't good for anything these days besides laying on their back and choking on a cock. That goes for my wife's crazy ass too.

I was pulling into the parking lot of the store after stopping to get my coffee and breakfast sandwich. I looked around the parking lot to see if I saw Terry's car and it was nowhere in sight. Her ass was probably going to be late since she was upset 'cause she had to come in. I knew all day today that she was going to be a problem. I walked in the store and headed straight to my office. As soon as I walked in, I noticed a time slip on my desk saying that Terry was going to be late. Not just a couple minutes late, but an hour and a half. I slammed my hands on the desk not really wanting to deal with these little bitches today. I hurried and looked over the cameras then got up from my desk to take a walk around the store.

Everything had seemed to be running well. All my staff was here except for Terry's ass. I had called her a couple of times, but she didn't answer me. I had a trick for her ass when she came in here. She would be at customer service with Haddy, and her ass had to stay later to cover her whole eight-hour shift. It was exactly eight days before Thanksgiving, and nine before our Black Friday sale. I was ready for it; that was the biggest sale of the year. I had to make sure I had everyone on for that day. I may even have to call the Welfare program to see if they had any more employees that need a job. Hell, I needed some more victims up in here.

After walking the whole store making sure everyone was in place, I made my way back into my office. I looked at the clock and an hour had passed that fast and still no sign of Terry. The sound of my office door opening brought me out of my thoughts.

"Sharp, I know good and damn well you did not put me at customer service with Haddy's dumb ass. Then I looked at the schedule and saw it says must work eight hours. I'm not staying here for no damn eight hours. I wasn't even supposed to be here." Terry snapped while walking into my office.

"First of all, don't come in here talking to me like shit. Secondly, I'm the boss and you're the employee. Sometimes, I think you forget that. No matter what we have going on you are still supposed to respect me." I retorted.

"You know what, Sharp, fuck you," Terry yelled then walked out.

I didn't care about her feelings. She was going to stomp her mad ass up to the customer service desk and work until seven o'clock. Since she came strolling in here at eleven o'clock. I had been letting her ass get away with too much stuff, and it was time to stop it. Before people start catching on to what we had going on. I didn't wanna piss her off, but I had to let her know who was the boss.

Sarai

After getting the kids ready for school, I was now walking out the front door to walk them to school. Thank God the school was right across the street from my house. I still had to walk Treyvon to the daycare on Banks Street which was fine. The thing I was going to regret was having to get on the bus to get to my car. I was hoping and praying that I could afford to get it towed to a mechanic today.

"Sierra, hurry up and help Sage put her coat on while I put Treyvon's snowsuit on."

"Mama…her coat is on already; we are waiting on you." She beamed. This little girl was a little too grown for her age. I swear she was up on everything. What I mean by grown is that she was so advanced for a seven-year-old.

"Ok suga…my fault. I thought y'all were still in the room. Come on. I'm ready."

As soon as I opened the door, a man was on my step about to knock. I looked up and noticed it was a tow truck dropping off my car. I was so happy. That way I could possibly get one of these hood mechanics to fix my shit right in front of my house.

"Are you Sarai Moore?" The tow truck guy asked.

"Yes…I am. Do you know who had my truck towed here?"

"I have all your paperwork ma'am. I was just paid to deliver it here. Can I get your signature, so they'll know the right person signed for it?" I signed the paper and then it dawned on me how did they get in my car. I was about to ask, but then I remembered he told me he didn't know anything. After signing the paper, I realized it had come from a mechanic, and it had over five hundred dollars' worth of work that needed to be done. Even them breaking into the car to fix it. I just laughed at the thought of that. Who the hell breaks into a car just to get it fixed. Sounds like some hood shit. I knew nobody did this but Tyrell. I just didn't understand why he was doing all this for me. This man didn't even know me. I took Sierra and Sage over to the school. Then hopped in my car to drop Treyvon off at daycare.

Once all that was done, I made my way back home to finish cleaning. I wanted to call Tyrell, but I was going to wait until I sat down to relax for a little bit. My phone ringing brought me out of my daze, so I picked up on the second rang.

"Bitch why didn't you work today?" Terry sassed into the phone.

"Well, hello to you too. I was having car trouble, but it's fixed so I should be back to work tomorrow as long as I have a babysitter. Why, what's wrong; what's going on over there?" I asked Terry.

"What isn't going on in here. I'm just over the bullshit."

"Things will get better; you know it's only hectic cause of the holidays. Well, I got to go. I'm cleaning the house. Call me when you go back on break." I said, and she sucked her teeth and hung up.

I didn't know what her problem was, but I was going to let it go. The minute I was about to lay my phone down it started to ring again.

"Hello…" I answered.

"Good morning sweetheart." Tyrell's voice boomed through my iPhone six plus.

"Hey, you!" I beamed with a big ass smile on my face.

"I wanted to see if your car got to you yet?"

"Yes, it's here. I was going to call to thank you as soon as I was done with the cleaning. You really didn't have to do that Tyrell."

"I know I didn't have to, but I wanted to. What are your plans while the kids are in school? Have you eaten anything for breakfast yet?"

"No… I haven't. I've been too busy trying to get the house cleaned before the kids get out. What about you?"

"I was hoping that I could come to get you and take you to Penn Queen Diner."

At first, I hesitated to answer, but then I figured what the hell. It's been a minute since a man had taken me anywhere. So, what the hell. I might as well see what he's about.

"I'm down…can you just give me forty-five minutes to get myself together? Would you like me to meet you there?"

"No, I'll be right outside your door in forty-five minutes. See you in a little bit beautiful."

Nothing else was said. I hung the phone up and made my way into my bedroom. With a big ass smile on my face. I didn't have much, but I was the type of person that could throw something cheap together and make it look like something. I decided on my black long sleeve pant body suit that I had just gotten from Rainbow a couple of days ago. I then paired it with a sweater poncho that I had got off the Macy's clearance rack.

Once I was dressed, I threw my box braids up in a high ponytail like Janet Jackson wore on Poetic Justice. Then I threw a little makeup on and was now ready to go. I slipped my feet in a pair of Moccasin Fringe boots. My phone alerted me I had a text message. I didn't even look 'cause I knew it was Tyrell. I just grabbed my purse, locked up my house, and walked out of the door. Before I made it to the car, Tyrell was getting out to meet me.

"Hey, Sarai…you look amazing."

"Thank you, Tyrell…you don't look bad yourself." I beamed while licking my lips. He had on that damn peacoat again, with a pair of jeans, wheat Tim's, and his dreads were styled perfectly. Not to mention his fresh line-up, and that damn full beard was to die for. I've never been interested in a man that wore glasses, but this man was fine as shit. I tell y'all no lie.

After he made sure I was comfortably sitting in the car, he closed the door then made his way around to the driver's side. I leaned over to open the door for him, and he smiled at me. We were riding in silence until Tyrell started to speak.

"So, did you get your babysitter situated?"

"I think she's cool now. So, I should be able to return back to work tomorrow."

"You don't have to. I already told Sharp that you weren't going to be there for a couple of days. So, go ahead and take tomorrow off too. I already made sure you were going to be paid."

"Alright, I can do that." I beamed.

We pulled into the parking lot of the diner. It seemed to be really packed. I didn't mind, though; that's how good the food was here. The sound of Tyrell opening my car door brought me out of my thoughts. I looked up at him and he grabbed my hand helping me out of the car. Once I was up and standing next to him, he shut the door and hit the button on his keys to lock the door. Tyrell then grabbed my hand and we walked into the diner holding hands.

"Dining for two?" The waitress asked.

"Yes…please," Tyrell said.

He put his hand on the small of my back, and we followed the waitress to our table. I slid in the booth and Tyrell sat right across from me. The waitress stayed and took our drink orders, and since we already knew what we wanted we gave her our orders.

"So, what will you be doing for Thanksgiving?"

"Well, usually I eat at the home where my mama is, but since they say she may be able to come home this year, I may cook at my house for me and her."

"Oh, you can cook?" I asked a little surprised.

"Yes, I can; my mama taught me well. What about you? What will you be doing?"

"It's just me and my babies, so most likely dinner will be at my house with just us. I don't have much family; my mama is a crack head, and my father, well, let's just say he could be the mailman for all I know. So, my kids are really all I have.

"If you want, you and the kids could come to enjoy dinner with me and my mama?" He asked, and I was in shock. I wasn't sure if I wanted to do that, but I would sure think about it.

"Can I think about it?"

"Of course, beautiful, just don't wait too long to let me know. So, I can make sure I cook plenty."

"Oh, I'll make sure I let you know in enough time."

"Make sure you do that beautiful," Tyrell said while winking at me. The waitress came out and laid our food on the table. Tyrell and I both started eating while enjoying each other's company.

Chapter Five

Terry

Pissed off had been my norm for the past couple of days. Why the fuck did I have to work for Sarai once again. She had been off for three days. It was supposed to only be two, but here it was she wasn't here again. I was furious and if I didn't need this job, I would have walked my ass right out of the door. I needed to find out what was going on with her. So, I was now on my way to her house. My phone rang stopping me from starting my car up.

"Hey, when you coming to get him?"

"Not right now Jessie, I got shit to do. The least ya ass can do is keep an eye on your damn son."

"Terry…you act like you the only one that has to make moves. How the fuck am I supposed to pay my child support if I can't go out and make some money?"

"Nigga, where the fuck is ya wife at. Tell her it's time for her to be a step mama for a change." I snapped right before hanging the phone up. I swear people were doing the most these days. Everybody felt the need to fuck with Terry. Nope, I wasn't having it. He should have thought about all of that before he got me pregnant. Now I was the baby mama from hell. I threw my phone in the passenger seat and peeled off.

Twenty minutes later, I was pulling up in front of Sarai's home. I saw her car sitting there, so I knew she was home. I parked the car and jumped out. I walked right up on her step and knocked on the door. The door opened, and her grown ass daughter was standing there looking at me like I was crazy.

"Mama…Terry is here."

"It's Ms. Terry little girl." She sucked her teeth and ran off. Me and that little demon seed had a love-hate relationship.

"Hey, Terry! What brings you here?"

"I came by to see how you were doing since you still hadn't been to work."

"Oh, come on in. I'm good. I was just enjoying a couple of days off until I got my car fixed and after school care for the kids. I have everything straight now. I'll be back to work tomorrow."

I walked into her house and I noticed that she had bags everywhere like she had just been shopping. I even noticed the big box over in the corner. It looked like an artificial Christmas tree. We didn't get paid until next week, so I wondered where she had hit the jackpot from.

"I see you've been doing some shopping. What you got paid early or something?"

"Nah…a friend of mine bought all of this."

"Bitch! That's why ya ass ain't been to work; you got a new man. What's the tea?" I said while flopping down on her couch.

"I've decided to leave it private until I find out what's really going on, but when I figure it all out you will be the first to know. So, how was work today?" Sarai asked while curving my whole question. That's ok; she didn't have to tell me, but my nosey ass would find out sooner than later.

"Oh, ok that's cool. Well, I'm happy for you; hopefully, he'll end up being your Prince Charming. That nigga spending cake already after a couple of days. You gave up the cookie already?"

"Nope… not yet. I'm not off that yet. I really wanna see where this goes. I've been with other men after Trey, but we were just hooking up. I'm ready for a long-term relationship, so I'm trying to take shit slow. Where's JJ at? Why didn't you bring him over here to play with Treyvon?"

"He's with his sucka ass daddy. Jessie called me right before I came here asking me when I was coming to get him. I told him I wasn't. I had shit to do. Shit, let him and his wife deal with his terrible two ass for a couple of days. Plus, I'm off tomorrow, so I need to find something to get into." Sarai just looked at me and shook her head.

"You stay giving that man hell."

"Well, he should have thought about all of that when he got me pregnant. Then decided to stay with his stuck-up ass wife."

"You knew he was married, Terry, and you continued to sleep with him. That shit was wrong on every level between the both of you. I know his wife is about sick of you. If you keep it up, they gone take JJ from you."

"Yeah, whatever. I'll blow they whole life up if they think about taking my son. Jesse knows not to play with me."

Sarai was getting on my fucking nerves, so I knew that was my cue to go. Whenever she started talking about my baby daddy and his wife the shit hit a nerve. I had to get the fuck out of here before I fucked her up.

"Do you want a glass of wine?" Sarai asked.

"No…I'm about to leave. I have to meet up with a friend of mine."

"Alright…well hit me up when you get home tonight."

I said my goodbyes then headed out of the door. I had to meet up with Sharp at the Red Roof Inn out in Cinnaminson. I didn't feel like being bothered with him tonight, but I needed my pussy ate to relieve some of this stress. I also needed some cash; my cable bill needed to be paid. I shot him a text letting him know I was on my way. I started my car up and peeled off.

After speeding down the highway I had just made it to my destination. I parked in my usual spot then headed inside. He was already there, so I just made my way to our usual room. I tapped on the door three times. When I walked in, Isabel was already sucking his dick. I thought to myself good 'cause I wasn't on that today. I didn't want that little pink pecker near me. All I wanted was for him to eat my pussy while Isabel fucked me in my ass with the dildo. Sharp got off watching us do all types of sexual shit to each other. The shit had him so amazed he would throw in some extra cash. After almost throwing up in my mouth watching her swallow Sharp's nut, I headed to the bathroom to freshen up a little, so I could get ready for the intense orgasm I came for. Once I was done, I was grabbing my cash and heading out. I hope Sharp didn't think he was fucking me. 'cause that shit wasn't happening. I was still mad at him; it would be a cold day in hell before I let that pink pecker touch me. That tongue gone be working overtime.

Tyrell

This little bit of time I had been spending with Sarai, I knew I wanted to see where this went. I knew we lived different lifestyles, but I also knew I wanted to do nothing more but help her. Cam said my ass was crazy for taking on a woman from the hood with three kids. He said it would be a lot for me, but every day I woke up it made me want her more.

I was at the center where my mama was about to have a meeting with the social worker to discuss bringing her home for the holiday. Sarai had agreed to come over with the kids. Cam and Keonna were coming over as well. So, for the first time in so long, I would have a house full for the holiday.

"Hello, Mr. McKnight. My name is Bella James, and I'm the new social worker taking over your mother's case."

"Hello, it's nice to meet you. What happened to Ms. Sinclair?"

"She moved up in the office so now she's my boss. She said if you would rather talk to her then you can give her a call, but I have your mother's file."

"No... you're good. I just wanted to know what happened to her."

"Oh…ok well let's get started. Have you seen your mother yet today?"

"No… I haven't but when I came last week it was like she didn't even need to be in here anymore."

"Ms. Sinclair and I had talked about that. We wanna see how she does home for the holiday. We wanna make sure that it doesn't trigger anything from her past. If she does fine, then we don't see a reason why you can't keep her home with you. You just would have to make sure she takes her meds like she's supposed to. A sudden slip-up could 'cause her to relapse, and then the behaviors will start. Which will make her a harm to herself as well as you. Are you ready for those type of responsibilities?"

"Ms. Bella James…I'm ready for anything that has to do with my mama. She took care of me and raised me to be the man that I am today. I owe her my life, so yeah, I would do anything for her to be home and her normal self. I noticed that in here it helped her cope with her sickness. This had been something that she had but didn't know. The death of my pops triggered it. That's crazy how you can live with something like that and not know it for years."

"Mr. McKnight…I'm afraid your mother has battled with bipolar schizophrenia for years but never told your father," Bella said. Hearing her say that had me pissed off. I know I was young, and she probably didn't want me to worry, but she still should have told me.

The thoughts of her been knowing had me thinking of so many incidents that occurred when I was little. I wonder were these the reasons I was always at Ms. Candice's house. I wonder if she knew about what was wrong with my mama. This shit was crazy, I was so upset I didn't even wanna see my mama today. I just wanted to go home and relax. Then I would go see Ms. Candice a little later.

"Bella…I'm aware of everything I need to do to bring my mama home next week. Now is there anything else you need to talk to me about?"

"No, not at all; just email us the times you will be picking her up and bringing her back. After we determine how she did, we will contact you about you taking her home permanently."

"Alright, and thanks so much for your time. Tell Ms. Sinclair I said thanks so much for all that she does for my mother."

After I was done with the meeting I headed straight out of the door with a lot on my mind. I just didn't know how to take the news I received today. I jumped in my car and right before I was about to pull off my phone rang.

"Hello," I answered not really in the mood to talk to anyone.

"Hey, you… is something wrong?" Sarai's soft voice spoke.

"Some family issues, but I'll be good. What's up with you? How's work been treating you?"

"It's ok…I don't think too many people like the idea of me being the new supervisor. I've been getting a lot of ugly stares, but other than that I'm enjoying a new position. I'm about to head out to lunch if you wanna meet up. You sound like you need to talk."

"I think I can use an ear. I'll meet you at the mall food court. I want some Chinese."

"Alright, I can use some of that too." I made my way to the mall. I was in Cherry Hill not even ten minutes away. I know I don't know Sarai all like that, but I feel like I can tell her everything. After making it in the mall parking lot I made my way to the food court side, then parked my truck. When I walked into the food court, I saw Sarai from a distance, but she wasn't paying attention. So, I eased my way up on her and grabbed her from behind then whispered in her ear.

"Hey beautiful."

"Hey, Tyrell." She cooed.

"You were all comfortable and rested your head on my shoulder. How did you even know it was me?" I chuckled.

"First of all, I saw you when you walked in. Then when you grabbed me and pulled me close to you, I smelled your cologne. If I didn't know who you were, I would have hit ya ass." Sarai giggled while turning around to face me. I then pulled her in for a hug while inhaling her sweet scent. After we stood in line and ordered our food, we made it to our seats.

"So, what's going on?" Sarai asked not wasting any time.

"I just found out that my mama has Bipolar Schizophrenic, and she been had it. All this time I've been thinking that whatever was going on with her triggered off when my pops died, but here it is years later, and she been had the shit. She just hid it from us. Why wouldn't she tell us, so we would know if something had happened to her?"

"Maybe she didn't want you to worry about her. Not to mention you were young; you wouldn't have understood. Being a mother will have you doing anything to make sure your babies are straight. So, don't be mad at her Tyrell. I'm sure she had her reasons. Just embrace the good news about her coming home for the holidays and enjoy her company."

I guess Sarai was right. I still was a little in my feelings, but I was going to try to push it behind me and focus on the future. Knowing that she was going to be home for the holidays did make my heart smile, and I couldn't wait. Having lunch and talking to Sarai about it made me feel a little better. This is why I needed her in my life; the shit just seemed so real even though we just started being cool. We talked some more and enjoyed our food until it was time for her to head back to work.

Chapter Six

Mr. Sharp

I had just come from Salad Works in the mall and on my way out, I noticed Sarai and Tyrell sitting having lunch together. I didn't know what the fuck was going on, but I hope she kept her mouth shut about what had been going on around the job. Then again, she was gone keep her mouth shut if she didn't wanna take her ass to jail. When I made it back into my office, Terry was sitting behind my desk.

"What the hell are you doing in here? You can't be doing shit like this. What if the store manager was with me?"

"Then I would have been acting like I was emptying the trash or something. Relax, I just wanted to know what's been up with Sarai. Have you noticed she's been acting different since she got that supervisor position? Whose idea was that anyway?" Terry looked at me with her lip turned up.

"Don't be looking at me all crazy; it wasn't my idea. Shit, if it was up to me, she would still be where she was begging for overtime to make ends meet."

"Why is that, so you can bribe her with sucking ya little ass dick." Terry snapped.

"Terry, you gone watch who you talking to."

"No, I'm not because I have a feeling you're the reason she got that position."

"No, I'm not…maybe she got it because she is fucking McKnight." I could tell the wheels were turning in Terry's head. I knew she would be good and jealous when she heard that shit. For some reason, she would always be jealous of everything Sarai did. Shit, I didn't know why; they both were single mothers that are struggling. The only difference with Terry is she has her son's father still around. Sarai's kids' father is dead.

"So, McKnight is the mystery man. That's why she didn't want me to know. Her stuck-up ass is fucking a real boss. I wonder how long this gone go on. Probably not that long if I have anything to do with it."

"What's wrong with her dealing with McKnight?" I asked curious about what Terry had in mind.

"Her messing with him will mess up our plans, and we can't have that happening."

"So, what do you have in mind?"

"Let the shit linger on until after Christmas then we should be able to make our move. It won't be smart to rob the safes until after the big sales right?"

"Yeah, but what are you thinking about?"

"Nothing, just let it all play out and leave her alone. Don't be trying to make her suck ya little dick no more. I want her and McKnight to get all in love then we will fuck they shit up."

I just sat there and looked at her like she was crazy. I hope her plan works out because I was ready to get this shit taken care of. The shit that my wife beats in my head every morning about me making more money and owning my own store has been weighing heavy on my mind. I needed to get up on some real cash. I don't have any idea how we gone rob this man for all of this money and get off scot-free. So, yeah, we had some planning to do, and I hope what Terry had in mind was going to work.

Later that night…

"Hey, daddy!" Joe Jr. came running into the living room jumping on the couch next to me.

"Hey son, what are you doing?" I asked a little-pissed off that he was bothering me.

"I came in here to see what you were doing. We never talk anymore since you're always working." Joe Jr. said in a sad tone.

"Well, son I have to work in order for us to eat and have a roof over our heads."

"Joe, stop feeding him that bullshit. Joe Jr. go-ahead to your room baby, and I'll be there to tuck you in real soon."

"Now why would you say that in front of him."

"Joe, shut up and finish watching TV. Like you always do when you're home. All you do is work, and if you not at work you pay us no mind. I'm beginning to wonder why the hell you're still here. You don't want anything to do with us, anyway, so why not let us go." Cindy snapped while walking off.

I knew she wasn't happy with my work hours, but I didn't know she felt like I didn't love her and Joe Jr. My wife was nagging and it kind of turned me off at times, but it didn't mean I didn't love her. I decided to turn the TV off and walked to the bedroom to talk to my wife. Cindy was lying on the bed up under the covers watching TV. I climbed in the bed and laid right next to her.

"I know I may be too much into my work, but that doesn't mean I don't love y'all. You and Joe Jr. are my world and I would never want you two to leave me. I promise I'll do better. Can you just bear with me hunny?" I assured her not believing a word I was saying myself. I knew I was a piece of shit, and I knew I would never change. I couldn't have my wife leaving me, so if I needed to try to do better than I would.

"I've always beared with you, and to be honest I'm getting tired of it. I love you with all my heart, but I refuse to stay here and let you do what you've been doing. I know there has to be other women since you haven't touched me in weeks. Just get it together, Joe, because you don't have much time before I decided to take Joe Jr. and leave." Was all she said before she turned over and drifted off to sleep.

Sarai

Thanksgiving Day…

The kids and I were at Tyrell's house getting ready for dinner. We had been spending time with each other for the past couple of weeks and the holidays were rapidly approaching. This year would be the best holiday I'd had in a minute. Now that my pay has gone up, I'll be able to get everything the kids want on their list. Even if I didn't have it, I knew Tyrell would make sure they get it. He had already bought the Christmas tree and the decorations. The kids told him he had to come over and help us decorate the house, and he agreed.

"What you in here thinking about?" Tyrell walked into the living room taking me out of my thoughts.

"Thinking about how today is going to be one of the best holidays I had in a while. I'm happy the kids are happy, and we owe it all to you. Thank you for having us, and for all you've done for us in this little bit of time."

"No thanks needed. Shit, I'm happy to have y'all I haven't had a big dinner in this house in so many years. To be honest, you and the kids give me life. Y'all have put a huge smile on my face each morning I get up. I haven't felt this way in a long time, and my mama coming home too. Yeah, I'm a happy man this year."

"Are you finished cooking yet?"

"Yeah…just about, thanks to you. I really appreciate you spending the night and helping me prepare this big feast."

"You're welcome boo…I didn't mind helping at all. I love to cook. What time will the transportation be dropping your mama off?"

"They should be dropping her off in about a half hour, and everyone else should be here in an hour. Where are the kids at?"

"They're in your movie room. I swear they are so amazed by this big ass house and everything you have in it. Are you lonely in this big house?"

"Sometimes, but most of the time I'm out working. I hope I won't be lonely much longer." He winked at me and made his way back into the kitchen.

I've been thinking hard about seeing where this will go between Tyrell and I. Then the shit I did with Sharp and getting caught taking out of one of the safes has me scared. Like how would he feel if he finds out about this shit. A knock at the door brought me out of my thoughts.

"Can you get that for me, Sarai?" Tyrell yelled from the kitchen. I got up and opened the door, and there was a beautiful woman that I assumed was his mother. He was the spitting image of her.

"Hello…you must be Ms. Sarai." The lady cooed while smiling at me.

"Yes... that's me and you are?"

"I'm Tyrell's Mama, Joyce. He has told me so much about you and your little ones." She said while holding her arms out to pull me in for a hug. I hugged her back inhaling her scent. After we hugged for what seemed like forever we closed and locked the door then made our way into the kitchen, so she could see Tyrell.

"Baby, you got it smelling really good in here. I guess mama taught you well."

"Hey, mama!" Tyrell beamed while pulling her in for a big hug followed by a kiss. She didn't seem like anything was wrong with her, but I knew from movies that people with those type of medical issues can act normal. Sometimes you will never know unless something offsets it. I had made a mental note to do some research on it, so I'll know what to do in any type of situation. Especially, if I plan to let her around my kids.

"Alright, help me out of this coat so I can help you finish up in here." His mama insisted.

"Mama…I'm hungry." Sage sad running into the kitchen.

"It'll be done real soon, princess. Would you like a banana while you wait?" Tyrell beamed while picking her up.

"Yes please…Mr. Tye." Sage cooed while smiling. He walked into the dining room while carrying her.

"She's a beautiful little lady you have there."

"Thank you, Ms. Joyce; she's my middle baby."

"I know…you have another girl and a little boy. Tyrell talks about the kids every time he comes to see me lately. I haven't seen him smile like that in so long. Please do me a favor and stay around. I don't want him to work his life away like his father did. He's at the age where he needs kids and a wife. Tyrell needs someone to share this big house with. He hates when I start talking about this to him, but that's only because the truth hurts. Tyrone let that job drag him down and leave his family in the process."

When she told me about him always talking about my kids, I couldn't do anything but smile. Usually, men acted funny when a female had so many kids. Not Tyrell' he acted as if he was falling for my kids while he was falling for me. I was torn, though, I didn't know how he would take the bullshit that I had been involved in.

"I like your son a lot, but I don't know if he can handle me and all my problems. I don't wanna come in and turn his world upside down."

"Chile, you're talking nonsense. Whatever it is it'll pass and you two will be happily ever after. He may be mad, but he will get over it. Just wait and see how everything starts to play out. Then when it seems like it is getting way too serious air everything out. Anything worth having is never easy to get. We all human and we come with issues. It's up to us how we deal with them. Now come on over here and help me put all the food in the crystal dishes so we can set the table. Do you know who else he's expecting?"

"Camron, Keonna, and Ms. Candice supposed to be coming over." I noticed the sudden look on her face when she said that, but I kept to myself.

"Good…today would be a good day to get this off my chest." Ms. Joyce said. I didn't like the sound of that, and I knew that Tyrell was so happy about today. I didn't want anything to upset him.

"Ms. Joyce, I know I'm new around here but whatever it is you need to get off your chest, if it's something that's going to upset Tyrell can you please wait until another time. He has been talking about how today is going to be one of the best holidays he has had in such a long time. You're going to be here for a couple days; just tell him another day please."

"Ok…baby you're right. I'll wait. Today is going to be overwhelming to see everyone anyway."

"Do you think you're going to be ok today?" I asked feeling a little concerned.

"I'll be fine baby…I'm just happy to have been able to make it over here to spend the holidays with my son. Last year, I was in a bad head space. Today, I feel like a new woman. The things medicine can do is surprising because, hunny, if you would have met me when I was a mess, you would be so amazed. They had tried numerous meds with me, but none of them work for me as good as this new one they have me on."

"Well, that's great. I'm glad you're doing good."

"Thank you, my love. Now tell me about yourself. Do you deal with your parents?"

"My mama is on drugs, and I never knew who my father was. My grandparents are dead, and I never had any siblings."

"Aww…baby, I'm sorry to hear all of that. What about your kids' father? Is Tyrell going to have to worry about him in any way?" She was being a little too nosey for my liking, but I knew she was just being a mother.

"My kids' father was gunned down about a year ago. Other than him being in the streets he loved me and his kids. He gave us the world. I just wish he would have gotten out of that street life and made an honest living for himself. Since he's been gone, I've been struggling like crazy, but for my babies, I'll do what it takes."

"Everyone is here…y'all can bring the food into the dining room. I already made sure the kids washed their hands. Come on before they jump me. I told them the food was finished. Y'all should have seen their faces when they got to the table and didn't see the food there." Tyrell chuckled.

"Ok, baby…we are bringing it in now." Ms. Joyce assured him.

I grabbed two dishes and made my way into the dining room. Cam was at the table; I swear he looked just like he did when we were younger. He just had facial hair.

"Rai…what's good with you ma. It's been a minute," he got up and pulled me in for a hug.

"Hey Cam, it's definitely been a minute. Hello ladies, I'm Sarai." I turned to speak to his wife and mama.

"Hello Sarai, I'm Keonna, Cam's wife. I've heard so much about you."

"Oh, did you…well you have to tell me what all you heard after dinner over some red wine." I beamed while winking at her. She was beautiful, and her skin was dark and smooth. She had a pregnant glow and it made her look amazing.

"We sure can suga." She beamed while smiling at me. After a couple more trips, Ms. Joyce and I had brought all the food to the table. Tyrell and I had cooked so much food it was crazy. Ms. Candice said our grace and we all dug in. Dinner seemed like it was going to be amazing. We all talked and got to know each other a little better, but the intense stare that Ms. Joyce kept giving Ms. Candice had me a little scared. I just wanted everything to be perfect.

Chapter Seven

Tyrell

Thanksgiving dinner was over, and Sarai wanted to go Black Friday shopping. I had never been shopping on Black Friday, so I was excited to see what it was about. Once we got to Walmart and I saw the lines I wanted to turn my ass back around.

"You mean to tell me you do this every year?" I asked Sarai while holding all these toys in my hand.

"I used to do it when Treyvon was alive, but I haven't done it in a minute. Money has been tight, so I really didn't do much shopping. This year since I got the pay increase, I'm able to."

"You mean to tell me all the money y'all had, you came out to get the sales?"

"Where is it written at that you can't catch a sale 'cause you have money. I'm all about saving a dollar no matter how much money I got. That comes from growing up in the hood and having nothing. Don't worry; if you stick around me long enough, I'll show you the ropes." Sarai laughed.

"So, this is the mystery man that got you acting shady." A voice from behind us said. I turned to see who it was as well as Sarai. The scowl on Sarai's face told me she wasn't in the mood for Terry's shit.

"Terry, don't start out here in front of all these people. Whatever goes on in my personal life has nothing to do with you or anybody else."

"I mean, we've been cool forever. What's the purpose of hiding what's going on?"

Hearing her say that had me wondering the same thing. Shit, we are out in public all the time. What's her reason for not wanting this chick to know what we had going on? I made a mental note to ask once we left here.

"I didn't hide shit from you, Terry. I just didn't tell you everything. Which it was up to me to tell you when I wanted to. You can be mad or take it how you want. I didn't want everyone at the job finding out since you can't hold water. I didn't want them thinking that I was getting any special treatment." Sarai retorted.

I didn't need to ask anymore; right then and there I figured it all out. I laid the toys down on the top of the cart and walked over to Sarai. I knew she needed me next to her. I noticed a couple days ago that my touch calms her. Lil' mama got an attitude on her, and most people don't know it until you tick her off. I walked up next to her and pulled her close to me.

"Shsssssss--- don't let her get you all worked up in here. It's not even that deep." I whispered in her ear while kissing her cheek. To my surprise, she grabbed my beard and pulled my lips to hers and kissed me right on the lips. This was a first and I enjoyed every bit of it. I had been wanting to do this for so long, but I didn't want her feeling uncomfortable since I was her boss.

"Mmm…I've been waiting to do that for a long time." Sarai cooed while licking her pretty ass lips.

"Oh…really, so why haven't you?" I asked curiously.

"I don't know. I guess I was just waiting for the right time, and this was a perfect time. Now go run tell that, did you do a video?" She snapped at Terry. Hell, I forgot her simple ass was still standing there. I was so caught up in that kiss.

"Sarai… you so corny for that. He probably doesn't really want you anyway. No man of his standards wants a chick from the hood with three fucking kids. He probably just wanna see how good that pussy is." Terry snapped.

Sarai got out of my hold and was on her way over to her, but I grabbed her. I guess this was the shit Cam was talking about; I wasn't use to this shit. People were looking at us like we were crazy. I just brushed it off and continued to calm Sarai down.

"Terry, I suggest you go on ahead somewhere with the bullshit before you regret it," I said in a low tone, but loud enough for her to hear me. She didn't say anything; she just told the girl she was with that she would wait for her outside."

"Tyrell you didn't have to do that. I had it covered." Sarai assured me.

"If I wouldn't have intervened, y'all would have been in here fighting Sarai. You have to learn how to ignore people and not let them get you off your square. Especially somebody like that filth bucket."

Sarai just sucked her teeth and turned her back to me. I didn't care about her little attitude. She was gone learn fucking with a boss ass nigga like me. Don't never let anybody bring you out of character out in public. We got shit to lose; that hoe don't.

"Alright, Tyrell I'm sorry. I didn't mean to embarrass you."
Sarai said just above a whisper.

"You didn't embarrass me beautiful. I just don't want you
out here fighting when it ain't even worth it. People gone
find out about us and so the fuck what. If you wanna switch
locations, then I'll put in for it later today."

"Nah…I'm good; Terry know what's up. I don't know why
she been acting funny lately. I may be quiet, but she knows
I can throw these hands."

"Well, it ain't gone be no throwing hands when you around
me. Now go ahead and start putting the stuff on the
counter." We had been so caught up in what was going on
we didn't even realize we were up next. After we laid
everything on the counter, the cashier started ranging it all
up. Once everything was rung and the total was six hundred
and fifty dollars, the look on Sarai's face told me she
overdid it. I wasn't going to let her pay for it anyway, so
she didn't have to worry about it. She went to pull out her
wallet, and I stopped her.

"Tyrell…you don't have to do that?" She assured me.

"I know I don't, but I want to. Didn't I tell you before when
you're in my presence let me do me."

"Ok…I'll let you have this one, but anything else we do
today promise me you'll let me handle it." I agreed with
Sarai but I couldn't see myself letting her pay for anything.
After everything was bagged, we got someone to help us
take the things to the car. After everything was loaded, I
opened the door for Sarai, and I made sure she was in there
comfortably before I closed the door. Then she reached
over to open the door for me when I made it around to the

driver's side. I loved every time she did that; my pops used to tell me all the time if a female didn't lean over to open the door for you after you opened it for her, she was selfish.

"Now we gone go to your house and wrap everything. Then we can take it and put it in one of your rooms. If I put it at my house the kids gone see it."

"Alright, I'm cool with that; what about the kids? Do we have to go pick them up?"

"No, not this early; they all probably sleeping. I'll call Erica later and see if she would be ok with keeping them longer for me. So, that way we can take a nap after we wrap everything. I know she'll be cool with that as long as the pay is good."

"Ok…well call her and tell her I got her when we pick the kids up."

Once Sarai called and made the arrangements with Erica. We headed to my crib to wrap all this shit. Then we were just gone chill until it was time to go pick the kids up later.

Terry

It had been a couple of days since the shit went down between Sarai and me. I couldn't believe this bitch tried to play me then her corny ass dude gone try to jump bad too. I had something for her ass and I can't wait until everything unfolds.

"Why are you laying there all evil and shit?" Jesse asked annoying me.

"Nigga, why the fuck is you still here. Ya wife probably wondering where ya hoe ass at since she got JJ."

"Man…let me get the fuck out of here. You be good for a little bit then you start ya bullshit. Make sure you be there to pick JJ up when ya simple ass gets off work tomorrow. My wife and I didn't make him. You and I did and it's not fair to her."

"Fuck you, Jesse…like you give a fuck what's fair to her. You just came over here and fucked my brains out on your lunch break while your wife watching our son. Tell me how fair that is."

"Shut ya stupid ass up, Terry. Why did you even have JJ? If you didn't want any kids."

"I never said I didn't want any kids. What I didn't want was to be raising a kid alone. I wanted you and the baby, Jesse, but you sold me a whole dream. If I would have known you weren't going to leave her then I probably wouldn't have kept JJ. Get the fuck out now!" I yelled while tears ran down my face.

"I'm sorry ma…I didn't mean to get you all upset." Jesse said while trying to pull me into his embrace. I put my hand up to stop him. All I wanted was him to get the fuck out of my house. This was a touchy situation for me being as though Jesse was the only man I've ever loved. Since he did me the way he did me. I have a don't give a fuck attitude. I don't know what's stressing me the most, my job or my fucked-up home life.

The sound of my front door slamming brought me out of my thoughts. How did this nigga have the nerve to leave here with an attitude? At least he goes home to someone while I'm left here all alone. It's times I wanna go over there and fuck up his marriage, but what good is that going to do. He had a whole baby on her ass and she didn't bounce. So, after a while I said fuck it. I wasn't gone try to sabotage their marriage anymore. The holidays were the time of the year I hated. Jesse always wanted JJ to spend it with him and his family. I would always argue with him about JJ going, but then I would end up letting him go. I didn't have any friends or family that I fucked with. So, that would be good and selfish for me to keep my son away from family and fun.

I had nothing to do today, so I figured I would just chill and try to get this plan together for Sharp and I. Banging at my door caused me to jump up of my couch. I had no clue who the fuck it was.

"Who is it?" I yelled in a loud tone.

"Hello Ms. Knowles, I'm from DYFS, the Department of Youth and Family Services." I opened the door up and there was a White lady and a cop standing in my doorway.

"How can I help y'all?"

"Hello Ms. Knowles, my name is Tracy Shepard, I was sent here because there was neglect and abuse reported."

"I don't know who contacted you guys, but I do not abuse or neglect my son." I sassed.

"May we come in and talk to you." I moved to the side and let them both in.

"Are you allowed to tell me who contacted you?" I asked with an attitude.

"They called anonymously, but I do have to look around your home to make sure it's a clean environment for Jesse Davis Jr." I took her on a tour. Thank God I had cleaned up because Jesse was coming over. My son had his own room with everything he needed. Jesse made sure he paid his child support and did whatever I asked for JJ."

"This place looks nice and clean, Ms. Knowles, but where is Jesse Jr. at right now?"

"He's with his father; we take turns keeping him during the week."

"Well, we were notified and told that you dropped him off at his father's house days ago, and you haven't called or came to get him. He also had a bad ear infection that you haven't taken him to the doctors to get treated. The daycare said they had been telling you that all he's been doing is pulling on his ear and crying. We actually got two different anonymous calls."

I sat down on the couch with an angry scowl on my face. I knew it had to be the daycare and Jesse's dumb ass wife Faith. That bitch. I can't wait until I see her stupid ass.

"Ok, so now what?"

"We have to do consistent pop-up visits. You have to take him to the doctor to get checked out tomorrow."

"I have to work tomorrow, and I won't be able to take him. So, his dad is going to have to take him."

"Ms. Knowles, I don't care who takes him, but with an attitude like that you need to be careful."

I thought about what she just said to me and I could kick myself. How could I say some dumb shit like that. I really sounded like me making money was more important than my son.

 "I'm sorry, Ms. Shepard. I'll make sure he gets to the doctor tomorrow. When will you be back?"

"I never tell. I just pop up, so just know I'll be seeing you soon." She said before she signaled the police officer to follow her. Once they left out, I marched my way into my bedroom and dialed Faith's number.

"You little bitch…I know you called DYFS on me. I hate you and Jesse and y'all are not getting my damn son. As a matter of fact, I'm on my way to get him now." I snapped then hung the phone up. I didn't even give her dumb ass time to speak. I hurried and threw some clothes on and headed out of the door.

Chapter Eight

Sarai

The closer we get to the holidays, the more work gets overwhelming. It had only been a couple of weeks into December, and this store was driving me crazy. Not to mention, Terry's attitude, and Sharp giving me the side-eye. I wanted to tell Tyrell so bad, but I didn't wanna get him involved in my work problems. Since he was the store owner, I still wanted work to be like it was before minus my run-ins with Sharp.

My name being called on the loudspeaker brought me out of my thoughts. It's been a minute since Sharp had even talked to me, so I hope he wasn't on no bullshit. I made my way to his office. When I got outside the door, I turned my nose up. I swear this fucking office smelled funny, and I hated entering. I opened the door and his fat ass was just sitting there looking at me all crazy.

"What do you need Mr. Sharp?"

"Close the door and lock it, Sarai." I did as I was told but continued to stand by the door.

"I need to get back to work, Mr. Sharp. You know it's the holiday season."

"Sarai…I noticed that you were walking around here with your nose up and your head held high. I don't care about you dealing with McKnight. As a matter of fact, how do you think he would feel about you trying to steal his money from his safes. Or, better yet, you sucking my dick from time to time." The tears started running down my face before I started to speak. This was why I didn't wanna make shit official with Tyrell. I knew my demons would creep up on me.

"Sharp please…I'll do anything you want me to do. You don't have to tell Tyrell anything. Please don't do that to me." I begged while walking over to him. When I made my way over to the desk, he backed the chair up and his dick was already out of his pants. The door busting open saved me. I backed away from him and ran out of the door. When I saw that it was Terry, I was so fucking upset. I didn't even wanna be at work anymore. I called Tyrell and told him I was on my way over to his house because I wasn't feeling good. He and his mama had the kids today, and I was grateful for the both of them. After clocking out and jumping in my car I peeled off and headed straight to Tyrell's house. I didn't even tell Sharp I was leaving; I just left.

Twenty minutes later, I was pulling up into Tyrell's driveway. Thoughts of what Sharp just said to me had me so messed up in the head. I wanted to grab my kids and just go home, curl up, and cry my eyes out. A tap on the window brought me out of my thoughts. I hit the lock button and Tyrell got in.

"Baby…what's wrong?"

"Nothing…I'll be ok. Sometimes around the holidays, I been feeling a little depressed about not having a family, but I'll be ok."

"Alright…come on. I have some bath water ran for you. When you finished, I'll have some dinner heated for you then we can just layup and watch some TV. Is that cool with you?"

"Yes, baby… that's fine with me."

When we made our way into the house, it was quiet, and the kids were nowhere in sight. "Where are the kids?" I asked.

"They're in the movie room with my mama. She done popped them some popcorn, they swear they at the movies. I told mama to keep them occupied while I take care of you." Tyrell said while grabbing my hand and pulling me in the direction of the stairs. No words were spoken; he led the way and I followed. We walked into his bathroom where soft music was playing, a bubble bath was running, and candles were surrounding the huge jacuzzi tub that sat in the middle of his bathroom floor. My eyes lit up, and I was so amazed. I hadn't had anyone do anything like this for me before.

"Tyrell, you didn't have to do all of this for me," I said just above a whisper. All I kept thinking about was the shit that Sharp had said to me earlier. I felt bad that I was leading this man on. I knew good and god damn well after he found out about me, he wouldn't even want my ass anymore.

"I keep telling you to stop telling me what I don't need to do for you. I got you ma, just let me take care of you." Hearing him say that made everything that Sharp said earlier go out of the window.

I couldn't do shit but kiss his lips. Our tongues entwined as we kissed for what seemed like forever. When he finally pulled away from me, he started to unbutton my shirt, when it was completely open. He then unfastened my bra and slid everything off. Tyrell peered at me, and it did something to me. I wanted this man, not just in a sexual way, but I wanted him in every way. Tyrell then proceeded to unbutton my pants. Next thing I knew, my panties were off, and I was standing in front of him in all my naked glory. The way he stared at me caused me not to speak at the moment.

"Come on, Sarai, get in the tub so I can wash you up." He grabbed my hand and walked me over to the tub then held my hand while I got in the hot steamy water.

"How's the water ma?" He asked making sure I was straight.

"Perfect baby, just the way I like it." Once I eased down into the water my body felt so relaxed, I couldn't help but close my eyes for a second to enjoy the feeling.

The minute my eyes opened back up, Tyrell was sitting there with a glass of red wine waiting for me. "Are you good ma? Do you want me to leave out while you soak? Then when you're ready for me to wash you up just call me."

"No…you don't have to go. Sit in here and talk to me. Hell, why don't you just get undressed and get in here with me." I said seductively.

"Are you sure that's what you want?" Tyrell asked to double check. I nodded my head, yes, and he started to undress. He kept his eyes on me while he stripped out of his clothes. Once he was completely naked, he climbed into the tub and sat across from me. He grabbed my feet and massaged them while we both enjoyed the hot water. All of a sudden a chuckle escaped Tyrell's mouth, while he proceeded to shake his head.

"What are you laughing at?" I asked curiously.

"I'm trying to make you feel good and I end up in the damn tub with you." I got up and eased my way over to him and straddled him.

"I figured why can't we make each other feel good tonight," I whispered in his ear while nibbling on his earlobe.

"*Mmm… Hmm…*I think that'll work." Tyrell responded back while biting down on his bottom lip.

I removed his glasses and set them on the side of the tub before I started placing kisses all over his face. I felt his dick rising up underneath me and I was getting turned on. I lifted a little, so I could slide down on his erection. The second I felt the head of his dick at my opening, I was already wetting him up with my juices. I eased myself all the way down having to get adjusted to his size since it had been a minute for me. Once he filled me all the way up with his dick, I was in heaven.

We both were so in tune with each other that my body was feeling things it had never felt before. I continued to bounce up and down on his dick in slow motion. While Tyrell was drilling up into me from the bottom. We were meeting each other stroke for stroke, while he kissed and sucked on both of my c cup breasts. My body just couldn't take it anymore. I moaned out in pleasure while having my first orgasm. Once I was finished shaking vigorously, I got my rhythm back and started moving up and down in a fast motion on Tyrell.

*"Fuck...*girl ride this dick." Tyrell moaned out in pleasure while I was trying to bring him to his climax.

*"Mmm...*baby, I think I'm about to cum again." I beamed while tightening up my pussy muscles on his dick.

"Goddamn Girl... let's just do this shit together." Tyrell barked while we both came long and hard.

I stayed on top of him with his dick still resting inside of me. My head was lying on his wet chest, while I panted trying to catch my breath. This shit was every bit of amazing, but then the thoughts of what transpired earlier came to mind and I was sad all over again. Tyrell lifted my chin to look me in my eyes.

"That was great baby, and I think it was what we both needed." I gave him a fake smile, and I guess he felt my uneasy feeling.

"I don't know what's going on, but we will be good ma. I know we are moving fast, but I'm fine with that. We both grown as hell Sarai. You don't have to worry about me being on bullshit, because that's not the type of guy I am. My parents have always told me that when I met the one, I would know, and I think I found her. It's gone be hard because we're still learning each other, but I'm willing to do whatever it takes." Tyrell said right before kissing me passionately. I probably should have aired everything out right then and there. I just couldn't bring myself to do it. I just pushed what I was thinking about to the back of my head and enjoyed our time together.

Tyrell

My mama had been staying at my house every weekend since Thanksgiving. The social workers wanted to make sure that she was well enough to bring home, and she actually was doing amazing. I think Sarai and the kids being over all the time helped a lot. I was walking into my house and I smelled my mama's famous sweet potato pie. I was coming to tell her the good news. That she was going to be staying home with me for now on. When I made it into the kitchen she was sitting at the table with Ms. Candice. They appeared to have tears in their eyes and I didn't know what the hell was going on. Before I got a chance to ask there was a knock at the front door. I walked to get it and it was Cam.

"What's up, bro? What are you doing here?" I asked looking confused.

"Man…I don't know. My mama just texts me and told me to come right over."

"Yeah, …something ain't right; they both sitting in the kitchen at the table crying." Before I got to say anything else, Cam was running into the kitchen. He didn't play about Ms. Candice, just as I didn't play about Joyce. Cam had me beat though.

"Relax Camron…I'm ok baby. You and Tye come to have a seat. Joyce and I have something to tell you both. Before I get started, you both have a choice to be mad and not wanna talk to us for a little bit but understand we're still your mother's. We made bad decisions when we were younger, and we both are sorry for that. Just know we love you with all our hearts." Ms. Candice assured us. I already wasn't liking this shit, so I just sat there and listened.

"A while back I had a breakdown and I had left Tyrone for a while. The time that I was gone he had met Candice. I was so afraid of him finding out about my sickness. I decided to stay gone for a little while until I got better. In the time I was gone I found out I was pregnant with you Tyrell. So, after I got my shit together, I made my way back home. Where your dad took me in with open arms. After we got settled and got our relationship back together, Tyrone gets a phone call from Candice, saying that she was pregnant with Cam."

"So, what exactly are you saying mama?" I asked getting annoyed about how she was talking around the situation instead of just getting to the point. Cam didn't say a word; he was just waiting just like I was.

"Tyrell, please baby calm down and let her tell the story. This is hard on both of us." Ms. Candice said in a sad tone.

I was growing impatient, I guess because I knew they were on some bullshit. Cam gave me the look which meant chill bro, so I did just that.

"Tyrell and Camron…you two are brothers." My mama managed to get out right before she started to cry hysterically. I looked at Cam and he looked at me. That's when the silence left him.

"Mama, what the fuck is she talking about. I thought John was my dad." Cam snapped.

"Camron, I know you mad and everything, but you better watch your mouth when you're talking to me. John is not your father, and that's part of the reason we got a divorce. I cheated on him with Tyrone. He found out about it, and we decided to put it behind us. Then when you came along

John couldn't deal with the fact that we found out that you weren't his. We all had agreed on just raising you like me and John's at first. John couldn't do it though; he said every time he looked at you, he saw another man. So, we just decided to call it quits. I'm sorry, baby. I didn't wanna interfere in Tyrone and Joyce's happy marriage, so we didn't say anything. Tyrone still took care of you financially and made sure to spend time with you and Tye together. Tyrell, that's part of the reason you were always at my house. Even though we kept this secret away from y'all we still made it so that you two would be tight. We practically raised you two together."

"Mama…I can't believe this bullshit." Cam said while jumping up and heading out of the door. I didn't say shit to my mama or Candice. I just followed behind Cam.

"Yo, bro hold up, where you about to head to?" I asked Cam.

"I need a fucking drink after hearing that shit. Let's go hit up one of the bars in the hood." I looked at him like he was crazy, but the way I was feeling I could use a drink or two my damn self. I hopped in my truck and Can jumped in his and we both peeled off.

After keeping up with Cam's speeding ass we ended up going to the old Pats. I hadn't been down here in a minute. Since Cam and I fucked up days. I had to laugh because we used to be acting a fucking fool back then. When Cam and I entered the bar, Cam saw a couple of cats that he knew at the pool table, so we walked on back.

"Yo, Cam and Tye…What's good with y'all." This dude asked, but I wasn't familiar with who he was. I looked at him lost for a second.

"That's Big Mike bro," Cam said.

"Oh shit…my bad bro, what's good with you?" I asked now knowing who he was; this nigga used to be fat and sloppy. Now he looks like a whole new person.

"You good my boy. I get that all the time, people are not used to seeing me this small. What's up? I haven't seen y'all out this way in forever."

"Life got in the way... now we need to drink our sorrows away." I chuckled.

I had to laugh at this mess. I just didn't understand why they didn't just tell us the truth. Their reasoning was dumb as fuck to me, and my feelings were so fucked up that my parents kept this shit from me. Granted, Cam and I are tight like brothers, anyway, and nothing's going to change our bond. I just feel like he got cheated like my pops left me his whole franchise and it should have been left to the both of us. I know Cam got his own shit going on, but he still should have had a piece of the pie. I wonder if my dad left him any money. A whole bunch of shit was going through my head. I just didn't know how to take the news.

"Here bro," Cam handing me a drink brought me out of my thoughts.

"What the fuck is this?" I asked after throwing it back.

"A double shot of Jameson," Cam chuckled. He knew I wasn't a big drinker, and I knew he planned on getting fucked up. I knew by now Candice had called Keonna. So, I shot her a text letting her know where we were. I knew when we left here, we were going to be good and fucked up.

Me: Sis we at Pat's, some bullshit went down, and I know we gone need a designated driver when we done playing pool.

Sis: I know. Candice called me. Just text me when y'all ready and keep my husband out of trouble Tye.

Me: I got you, sis…

After I was finished texting Keonna, I shot Sarai a text letting her know I needed her tonight. So, I was going to get dropped off over her house. She said ok, she'll see me later, and be safe. I smiled and slid my phone in my pocket and threw another double shot back.

Chapter Nine

Mr. Sharp

It was December the fifteenth, exactly ten days before Christmas, and the store was in an uproar. Terry kept missing work because of the stuff with her son. Sarai didn't say anything to me; she got her schedule from the supervisor. It got to the point she wouldn't even call out to me. The shit wasn't working for me, so I had no choice but to call McKnight to let him know I couldn't work in these conditions. So, he wanted to have a meeting today. I had to call Terry to tell her she had to attend. I was glad that she was able to make it. I didn't want her getting fired. Once the meeting was finished between all the members of the store McKnight dismissed everybody except for us four.

"So, what's been going on in here," McKnight asked while looking around the room.

"I feel like since she's been dealing with you her nose has been in the air," Terry said.

"First of all, whatever I do outside of work has nothing to do within here. You're the one that has a problem with my relationship, which I don't know why. I thought we were cool, Terry, but the way you've been acting tells me a lot about you." Sarai sassed.

"Terry, our relationship doesn't have anything to do with work. If you don't wanna work here I can always relocate you. I've noticed you've been missing a lot of days anyway. What's been going on?"

"I'm going through a little issue with my son, but it's almost taken care of." Terry snapped.

"Well, since you're going through something, I'ma take you off the schedule until you get it situated. It's Christmas time and I can't afford to be having my business not run properly. This is the time of year the most money is made. I need everybody at work plus extra people. When you get it handled let me know and I'll put you back on schedule." McKnight said, and I could tell by the look in Terry's eyes she didn't like the shit.

"Now Sharp, what's your problem with Sarai?"

"The only problem I have with her is the communication. When she gone be late, call out, or go on break I need to know. She doesn't like me and that's fine, but we still have to communicate in the workplace. That's all; other than that Sarai is one of my great workers." I said while laying it on thick.

"Is there a reason why you're doing these things Sarai?" McKnight asked. I made sure to look at Sarai with a half-smirk on my face. I knew she wouldn't say anything bad because I had the advantage over her right now.

"Nah…I told you this is the time of year I go through personal issues, but from here on out, I'll get it together, now can I go?"

"Yes, everyone may go, but remember this is the week the store has the most business. Sharp, I'ma need you and Sarai to keep it professional. My store needs to run properly. If y'all have any call-outs let me know and I'll come in and help. I know this week is going to be a lot, so if it's too much for anybody to handle just let me know and I'll cover their shift."

Tyrell was just like his father, but I didn't think I could run any bullshit past him. The way that he looks at me I could tell he doesn't care for me He's looked at me the same since he's met me. I wonder why he didn't fire me yet. After we all left out of the office, I watched him and Sarai walk off together, He tried to keep his hands off of her, but he couldn't help himself. I just shook my head and walked in the opposite direction. I walked into my office making sure to lock the door since I knew McKnight was here.

"It took you long enough to get in here," Terry said causing me to jump.

"Terry, what the fuck did I tell you about coming in here? McKnight is in the building."

"Sharp, don't get your draws all in a bunch. All I wanted to say was we need to get up on this plan right now. I need some cash. I have to get the fuck away from here. Jesse and Faith are trying to take my baby. I can't have that Sharp."

"So, what are your plans? You really trying to run away with your kid. That might not be a good idea, Terry, especially if he's trying to get custody."

"Sharp, I didn't come in here to hear you tell me what's right and wrong. If you not ready to make a move by Christmas Eve, I'm going to put my own shit in motion. Now fuck with me if you want to, Sharp, and I can show you better then I can tell you." Terry snapped and walked right out of the office. While she was walking out, Cindy was walking in. *Fuck,* I thought to myself. Cindy and I had been doing good. She finally told me that she was tired of seeing Terry walking out of my office whenever she arrived. Terry smirked at her on her way out like she always did. Which is why my wife suspected us messing around.

"I came to bring you lunch, but I see you were busy," Cindy said while throwing the bag of food on the floor and walking off. I ran after her. When I finally caught up to her, I grabbed her arm.

"Cindy wait …it's not what you think. She is one of my employees. I'm going to have to deal with her. Now stop acting like this and listen to me. I have never had anything with that young lady but a working relationship."

"Joe…I would believe you if every time I come up here, she wasn't looking at me smiling. If a working relationship is all it is tell the little black bitch to stop looking at me like that." Cindy yelled.

"Ok, my love I'll do that. Now please come back and have lunch with me." Cindy agreed to come, and we headed back into my office. I opened up the Chick-fil-A she brought me and noticed she didn't have anything for herself.

"Where's your food at?" I asked.

"I wasn't hungry. I had a late breakfast after I took Jr. to school."

"Oh, ok. Well, I'm hungry; you came right on time. McKnight was just here, and we had a meeting."

"What was the meeting about? It needed to be about you getting your own store or getting more money. You practically run this store; he doesn't do shit but sit back and collect his money. Is he giving you a Christmas bonus? His dad used to; this young man doesn't know anything about running a business." Cindy fussed. McKnight still gave us bonuses. I just never tell Cindy about it. I need to enjoy some money for myself.

"Hunny please; everything is going to change real soon. Just trust me, it's going to take time but I'm going to make it work. So, can we talk about something else please. Who wants to talk when they have a beautiful woman in their presence? Cindy got up and locked the door then walked back over to me and sat on my lap. We talked and enjoyed each other's company until she got on her knees and gave me the best head I've ever had from her.

Terry

The shit that has transpired between me, Jesse, and Faith was getting out of control. To the point that Jesse didn't even wanna deal with me anymore. Him and Faith had requested full custody saying that I was unfit. Then Tyrell McKnight took me out of work. Yeah, I know his whole name. I did a whole search on that nigga. He thought he was the shit, but I was gone rob that nigga, and I had another surprise for him and his precious Sarai.

The social worker stayed on my ass, and she knew I wasn't working at the moment. So, she wanted to know how I would be supporting JJ. I had to tell her the only reason I wasn't working was because of all this court shit. I was getting child support for my son, and Jesse used to help me in anyway. Now that he is applying for full custody, he hasn't sent me a child support payment. I don't have shit since I haven't been to work. So, now they have JJ all the time. This is not a good look for the DFYS worker.

I swear I was ready to lose my damn mind. Not to mention Sharp still hasn't gotten back to me about how we gone make this robbery. I need this cash as soon as possible. A knock at my front door brought me out of my thoughts. I jumped up to answer the door hoping that it wasn't this damn social worker. When I pulled the door open, it was Sharp's fat ass.

"I hope you here with a plan." I sassed while walking away from the door.

"When will you be back to work? It's hard to put a plan in motion and your ass didn't call McKnight back to let him know you want to be back on the schedule. If you can, come back to work Christmas Eve and the day after. Then maybe I could make it so that we will have to do the drop. Since it's the holidays and no one is coming to pick it up. I'll have McKnight thinking it's me and Casey, but it'll be you and I."

"That sounds like it may work. Are you sure you down with this or are you going to bitch up?"

"I said I was going to do it. Cindy is on my back about me making more money then what I'm making."

"Well, maybe if you weren't always fucking off with young, Black girls you would have money." I giggled while walking into my kitchen to grab me water.

"Now if I stop doing that your money supply would be cut off."

"Joe…I know damn well I ain't the only one you be paying for sex. You haven't touched me in weeks, and I know that little wife of yours ain't satisfying that big ass sex drive ya nasty ass got."

"Since you talking so much shit, you might as well come to ride this cock for me before I head back to work."

"You already know if the cash is right, I got you." I didn't feel like wasting my time on Sharp's ass with his little ass dick of his. I needed all the coins I could get at the moment, so I guess after he disappointed me, I would shower and play with my toys.

****

"Wake ya hoe ass up," Jesse yelling woke me up out of my sleep.

"Nigga, what the fuck are you doing in my house making all that damn noise. Don't you see I'm trying to sleep?" I hollered while rolling back over.

"So, you are prostituting now Terry?" Jesse barked.

"What the hell are you talking about Jesse?"

"Don't play with me ma. I saw that fat ass White man in here earlier. I came to bring the baby to see you, but when I saw that sick shit I walked right back out of the door. I was gonna fuck you up, but I was like nope. I ain't gone fuck up the chances of getting my son. The shit I saw today told me everything I needed to know. Faith kept saying ya ass was nasty, but I didn't pay her any mind. I'm glad I stopped fucking ya nasty ass."

"First of all, that's what you get for letting yourself in my damn house. Secondly, fuck you and ya ugly ass wife. You just fucked me a month ago, and guess what, I been fucking that fat ass White man." I giggled while waving him off. I wasn't gone argue with him about what I do with my pussy.

"Bitch, you nasty as fuck for this shit."

"Jesse, what you really mad at, huh? You mad cause the pussy that you be wanting from time to time has violated you? Is that what it is? I use protection baby; we still can do it. Come on, let's do it now; he doesn't satisfy me like you do." I cooed while opening my legs wide giving him a good view of my pussy.

"Man…Terry go ahead with that bullshit."

"Why not; you know you can't get enough of this good shit. That's why you won't leave me the fuck alone. You say you want JJ, but when you take him how you gone get over here to see me. He was your excuse; now you not gone have one." He looked at me while shaking his head. I knew he wanted to fuck me, but he was being hesitant. I guess he was growing tired of hurting Faith's feelings.

"Nah…Terry I'm good on you ma. I don't want nobody but my wife." Jesse said while turning and walking out of my house. My heart broke in a million pieces. This was the first time he had ever said anything like that to me. We always argued and fought, but we always got it together. I jumped up and looked out the window and watched him pull off. I felt so defeated I just locked my door and climbed back into my bed.

Chapter Ten

Sarai

It was Christmas Eve and we were all dressed alike in the same pajamas. Tyrell and his mother were still going through it, but I noticed today he was at least talking to her. For days he hadn't said anything to her. I had a long talk with him letting him know he can be mad about it, but what's done is done. This is the first Christmas they've spent together in years, and he needed to make an exception.

"Baby, what you in here doing?"

"I just finished wrapping your last gift. I'm glad I finished before you came back in here. I told ya, mama to make you stay in there."

"Now you know you can't keep me away too long." He chuckled.

"Yeah…I've noticed." I cooed.

"Ain't nobody told you to put that good stuff on me," Tyrell said while walking over to the bed and climbing on top of me.

"Boy…get ya horny ass off me. Before the kids come in here."

"They not coming in here; mama making Christmas cookies with them. While they making cookies why won't you let me taste ya cookie really quick? You know it won't take me long at all." Tyrell said while licking his lips.

"You so damn nasty." I giggled while pushing him off of me.

"Wait, where are you going?" Tyrell asked sitting up on the bed.

I walked over to the door acting like I was going out of it, but instead, I locked the door. I turned around and slid my bottoms down.

"Nowhere…just locking the door so you won't be interrupted while you're enjoying your cookie." I cooed. Tyrell got up and walked over to me. He then lifted me on his shoulders and leaned me up against the wall for support while he devoured my pussy. Tyrell knew how to please my body; he licked, slurped, and kissed on my cookie making me squirm. I was so scared he was going to drop me, but he balanced me on his shoulders while fucking the shit out of me with his tongue.

"OH MY GOD! Tyrell just like that baby…just like that." I moaned out in pleasure, while he feasted on my kitty sending my body into pure ecstasy. He was eating my pussy so good, I felt tears starting to run down my face. The way he was pleasuring me was doing something crazy to me. I felt this funny feeling in my stomach and it caused me to try and close my legs, but Tyrell wasn't having that shit.

"Nah ma…leave them legs open and let me bring this nut up out ya." He groaned between licks.

"Oh, sss---shit. I'm cumin', baby," I said as my juices ran out of me. I felt weak as shit, as Tyrell brought me down from his shoulders. He carried me to the bed and laid me down. I rolled right over and laid there. The way I was feeling I was going to take a little nap. I felt him get up from the bed I guess he went into the bathroom. When he came back into the room, I felt him wipe me down then cover me up. I then felt him kiss my cheek before he headed out of the room. I was living the life. I had definitely found me a boss for the holidays. I just hoped my past didn't mess up what we had going on.

"Wake up baby…wake up; the kids are sleeping now, so we can put all this shit they got under the tree," Tyrell said waking me from my deep slumber.

"What time is it?"

"It's one o'clock in the morning. I put ya ass out for a minute."

"Oh, my goodness, why didn't you wake me up. I missed everything." I said with a frown on my face.

"I wasn't gone wake you up. You been so tired from work and running around finishing the last-minute Christmas stuff. The kids were fine; my mama helped them bake cookies for Santa. Then they all fell right to sleep.

"You and your mother are so good to my babies; they really haven't had a relationship with my mama cause of her drug addiction. So, I'm grateful for your mama; she loves them, and they love her. My kids are going to have a great Christmas thanks to you two."

"I told you no thanks needed. When I said I wanted you that meant I wanted your kids too. Y'all being here with me is the best Christmas gift I've had in years."

"Aww…I'm happy that we make you happy. Give me a kiss." I said while leaning in to kiss his soft lips.

"Alright, now you better cut it out before the kids' gifts don't get under the tree. Come on so we can get this done. I opened the door to the guest room and looked at all that shit and turned my ass right back around. They have so much stuff my whole Livingroom gone be covered with gifts. You not even gone see the damn tree." Tyrell said while shaking his head.

"Well, you the one that did it. I was done with they little asses and you wanted to keep getting them shit. So, that's why your living room is going to be packed with gifts."

"Nah…that was all you; all I did was pull my wallet out to pay."

"Yeah ok, Tyrell…move ya lying ass." I said while nudging him. We both got up and headed to the guest room to grab all the presents to place the gifts under the tree.

After making a million trips back and forth from the room to the living room, we managed to get all the gifts in the living room. It was so many we couldn't even fit them all under the tree. One half of Tyrell's big ass living room was filled with gifts.

"Well, damn did y'all buy them kids enough stuff?" Ms. Joyce said as she walked into the kitchen to get something to drink.

"Your son did all this. I kept telling him they didn't need all of this, but he wouldn't listen to me."

"I'm sure it was him."

"Mama you supposed to be on my side; how you gone agree with her."

"I mean, I love you baby, but I believe everything she just said to me. Plus, I'm her best friend right now since she gave birth to my new three beautiful grandbabies." Ms. Joyce beamed.

"Since you put it that way, I'll let you slide." Tyrell smiled.

He and his mama really adored my kids and this is why I've come to the conclusion that later on today after Christmas dinner I'm going to come clean and tell him everything that's been going on in the store. I was even going to explain to him about the time I stole out of the safe, bills were piling up and I hadn't received my first paycheck yet. So, I decided to take the money from the store. I swear I was going to put it back when I got my first paycheck, but me being stupid I didn't; then later on I found out that Sharp's fat ass had me on camera. I cried like a baby when he showed me the video. He told me all I had to do was get on my knees and blow his mind real quick and he wouldn't have me arrested. I did as I was told and have been ever since. I couldn't go to jail and leave my babies. I was all they had.

"Baby, you good over there?" Ms. Joyce asked. I looked around and didn't see Tyrell.

"I'm ok mama; just thinking of something from my past.

"If it's something that you need to get off your chest, make sure you do it before it's too late. Especially if it's a serious situation. I know my son loves me, but our bond will never be the same because of the secret I kept from him. If you love him tell him before it's too late. The love that he shows you and your kids is genuine. I've never seen him like this with anybody. Hell, I think you're the reason he didn't kick my ass clean out his house after I told him my secret." She giggled to lighten the mood, but I knew she was dead serious. Tyrell has gained a soft heart since we've been in the picture.

"I know y'all not in here talking about me." Tyrell came walking back in the living room with more gifts.

"What the hell is that Tyrell? I thought we were done bringing gifts in here?"

"That was just the kids' things. This is your and mama's stuff."

"Aww…son you got me some gifts."

"Of course, mama…I may be a little upset with you but you're always gonna be my favorite lady." Tyrell said while walking over to his mama and pulling her in for a hug and a kiss. The sight before me almost had me in tears. I wanted to see my mama just to say hello. I miss her so much, but she just can't seem to get herself together. I didn't even know I had let a tear escape my eyes until I felt Tyrell wiping it off.

"What's the matter, Sarai?"

"I miss my mama, Tyrell, and I wanna see her today even if it's just to say hello."

"Well, we can make that happen tomorrow before dinner. We can leave the kids here with mama and Ms. Candice. I wouldn't want to take them since we not sure what we are walking into. Do you know where she lives?"

"I have her last address."

"Ok… cool don't cry we going to see her," Tyrell assures me while pulling me in for a hug.

Since we finished setting up the tree, we all decided to go ahead and get a nap in before the kids woke up. I knew Treyvon's little butt would be the first one up. He was so excited.

Tyrell

Christmas Morning…

I woke up in a great mood this morning. The kids were already up and running the house. I just sat back and watched them rip open their gifts. They were so happy and excited it warmed my heart.

"Mr. Tye… when are you going to open up your gifts that we got you?" Sierra said while sitting on the couch next to me.

"I'll open up my gifts when I'm finished watching you open all of yours. Now get back over there and finish." I said right before I started to tickle her. I loved this little girl so much; she was a little sassy girl, but so sweet at the same time. All of Sarai's kids adapted to me so well. It was like I was meant to come right into their lives, and they completed mine. There was no doubt in my mind they weren't what I needed.

"What are you sitting over here thinking about?" Sarai asked.

"How I met y'all right on time, and I feel like in this short time we were meant to be."

"Aww…baby I feel the same way. I haven't been this happy in so long and I owe it all to you." Once those words left her mouth, we shared a passionate kiss, until Treyvon came over patting on my leg. He wanted to show me his new truck. I swear this little nigga never said anything but two words since we met, but today he was full of surprises. I guess he used to me now.

After the kids opened everything and we ate breakfast, Sarai and I were headed out the door to go see her mama. I figured we would go while my mama and Candice were cooking dinner. Today Cam and Keonna were coming over as well. My boy and I finally talked and decided we couldn't be mad at our mothers forever. We already carried ourselves as a family, so the news wasn't going to change anything. He also called me this morning and told me that our pops had left him a letter, and Candice had given it to him this morning. My pops had left him a lump sum of money. He went on to say how he knew that taking over his franchise wasn't for Cam, so he left him money to do whatever he wanted to do with it. The shit was crazy how everything went down, but we will pick up the pieces and keep it going. I'm just glad that my blood brother happened to be someone that I had already considered a brother.

"Alright, babe we can pull off now. The last address I have on her is an old apartment building out East Camden across from Davis Elementary School. Do you know where that is?"

"I think I know that area." I peeled off and headed straight in that direction.

I noticed that Sarai was fiddling with her fingers. Something that she does when she's nervous. I grabbed her hand with my free hand and begin to rub it. I knew this was going to be an emotional moment for her.

"I haven't seen her in so long Tyrell."

"I know, baby, but you're not going to feel complete today until you see her. It might not be the way you wanna see her, but at least you get a chance to see her. Why haven't you tried to find her in a while?"

"I guess it just hurts me to bad to see her like she is, but today seeing you and your mama made me wanna see mine. I miss how holidays used to be when I was little before she started her bad habits."

We were now pulling up to the old apartments, and the shit looked terrible. I'm so glad we didn't bring the kids along. I hopped out and opened the door for Sarai then helped her out of the car. Sarai held my arm tight and stayed close to me. When we entered the building, it was a strong stench of piss lingering in the halls. Trash all over the place, and niggas chilling like it was normal. One dude gave me a head nod while the other just stared at Sarai and me. I gave them all a head nod and kept it moving. I figured we were at the apartment when Sarai stopped. She just stood there and peered at the door. I went ahead and knocked for her. The smell in this hall was starting to get to me. After the third knock on the door, it finally flew open. The lady that opened stood in shock for a minute as she kept her eyes on her daughter.

"Hey, mama!" Sarai spoke.

"Hey, baby…come on in." Sarai headed in and I followed right behind her.

"Mama, this is Tyrell…Tyrell this is my mama, Sandy."

"Hello Tyrell, it's nice to meet you. I wish I would have known you were coming. I would have cleaned up a little." She said with a half-smile.

"Hey Ms. Sandy, it's nice to meet you." I beamed.

"I didn't know I was coming, mama. How have you been?"

"I've been maintaining baby girl…trying to get my life back on track. How're my grandbabies doing?"

"They are doing great mama. What are you doing today?"

"Nothing like always. I've been cooped up in this apartment trying to stay out of trouble. It's hard as hell but I been doing good. I know you may not believe but I swear I'm trying Sarai. I'm tired and I miss you and my grandkids. I haven't called or came around because I'm trying to get my shit together all the way." Sandy said.

"I understand, mama, but if you really want help you may need to go away to a program. You just staying closed in and trying to kick this shit alone can be hard. You don't have to be alone. I'll help you if you need me to." Sarai assured her.

"Baby…I know you got your own life going on. You can't afford to worry about me. I don't need you stressing over helping me when I let you down so many times." Ms. Sandy confessed.

"Mama, if you're serious about getting help, then I don't mind helping at all. You know regardless of what you got going on, you're still my mama and I love you with all my heart. I love more than anything in the world for you to get clean, so your grandkids can meet the real you. Before your life took a change for the worst. You were the best mother to me when I was younger." Sarai encouraged her mama.

I could tell that their conversation was getting a little heated and the tears were going to start to fall. I didn't wanna see that, so I figured I would jump in right quick.

"Ms. Sandy, I'm having a big Christmas dinner at my house. You're welcome to come along." I assured her.

"I wouldn't wanna impose."

"You wouldn't be a bother at all mama. The kids are there having a great time. Plus, Tyrell has plenty of room. I would really love for you to join us."

"Ok…let me go get dressed. I promise I won't be long." She said while running off to her room.

"Tyrell…thank you so much. I swear you were heaven sent." Sarai said while pulling me in for a hug. I couldn't help myself. I had to kiss her sexy ass. We were kissing until we heard her mother walk back into the living room.

"Don't stop on my account. I was just trying to find my other shoe." Ms. Sandy said and we both burst out laughing.

"I got you baby, and whatever makes you happy I'm all for it. Now, come on before my mama starts calling wondering where the hell we at." Ms. Sandy and Sarai were heading out of the door and I followed right behind making sure to lock up. If Ms. Sandy had plans on getting help, her first step would be to move out of here.

****

Dinner was finally over, and we all were just sitting around drinking spiked Eggnog. Ms. Sandy seemed to be having a great time with the kids. I figured she should spend the night. I just hope I didn't regret it and wake up to shit missing in the morning. I never grew up around a drug addict, but I've watched enough on TV.

It was getting late and the kids needed to be bathed and put to bed. I took Treyvon in my bathroom, and Sarai had the girls in the guest room. That way, we could get this done fast. Our moms were tipsy off the Eggnog still downstairs talking. Cam and Keonna had left to go home since they were tired. Sarai and I were tired as fuck, too, which is why we were trying to get the kids to bed so we could relax. After I was done helping Treyvon, I picked him up and we headed to the guest room.

"Hey, my little suga man." Sarai cooed while taking Treyvon out of my arms. I entered the guest room and the girls were already in the bed.

"Did y'all have fun today?" I asked.

"Yes, Mr. Tyrell and thanks for all the gifts you bought me, my brother and sister." Sierra cooed.

"You're welcome princess and thank you for being a big girl and helping your brother and sister all day."

"You're welcome too."

"Alright…now go head to sleep, . Y'all had a long day," Sarai assured them. After we made sure the kids were straight, we headed to check on our mamas; they both had gone to bed. So, Sarai and I did the same. Today was a great Christmas and the rate Sarai and I was going we would spend many more together.

Chapter Eleven

Mr. Sharp

Christmas was actually a success in the Sharp house, but now today was the reality of it all. I had sent Terry with the money, and we were going to meet up later. I had been on eggshells all day scared that McKnight would be on to us. From the looks of things Sarai had him occupied, so I didn't have to worry about that.

"Mr. Sharp, do you know that Terry did a no call, no show," Casey asked being nosey as usual.

"Yes…I already wrote it down. I'll tell McKnight about it tomorrow. I know he's enjoying the holiday with his family, so I didn't wanna bother him with that."

"Ok…I just wanted you to know." Casey said.

I knew she would be getting a little suspect. I also knew she would call McKnight when shit wasn't going right in the store. I had just recently found that out. So, I had to keep a close eye on her. I walked into my office and sat at the desk just looking through my phone wondering when Terry was going to call. She was supposed to call me to let me know she was in the clear. Then I would meet up with her when I got off.

"You fat sloppy mutha fucka!" McKnight came barging in my office. Before I could say anything, I was being pulled from behind the desk. He sent blow after blow straight to my face.

"Wait a minute, McKnight, wait a minute. It wasn't me; it was all Terry's idea." I managed to get out right before he kicked me right in my face.

"Chill bro…let that stupid asshole tell you what the fuck Terry's idea was. Pick his fat ass up and sit him back behind the desk."

"Speak ya fat bitch." Tyrell grimaced.

"It was all Terry's idea to rob you. She'll be calling me soon for me to meet up with her. Then we were going to split the money and blame it all on Sarai." I said right before he hit me in my mouth again.

"Where does this raggedy bitch live? You two stupid asses done fucked with the wrong one. I wasn't even coming here for that. I was coming because I got that fucking video of you making Sarai suck ya nasty ass dick. At first, I was about to fuck her up then I realized that she was crying in the video. What the fuck was that all about Sharp?" Tyrell yelled, causing me to jump.

"One day I caught her stealing out of the safe, and I've been threatening to have her arrested if she didn't do what I told her to do."

"We got us a perv ass nigga here. So, who else ya ass been sexually harassing up in here?" The other guy that was with McKnight asked.

I hesitated to respond, and another blow went to my head.

"All the girls that come in for the welfare program." McKnight walked over to the computer and looked something up. When he was done with that, he called the store security.

"I got ol'girls address. Let's go get her ass before she tries to run off with my damn money. Cause I bet she was never going to call this fat ass dummy."

"Yeah…she a hood chick; she was ready to bail on him."

"Hey, Mr. McKnight…what do you need me to do?" Corey walked into the office.

"I want you to stay with him until the cops come. They already know what they are coming for. Tell them the store owner will be in soon to follow with the report."

"Alright, boss…what do you want me to do when they take him out?"

"Nothing, I already talked to Casey; she'll be running the store in his absence. After they come and take his fat ass, give me a call." Once McKnight left out Corey hit me again.

"That's what ya fat ass get. I knew sooner or later somebody was going to catch up with ya ass. I hope they rape ya fat ass while you locked down. Your kind is a really fucked up individual. You use people's weakness against them to take advantage."

Corey was right. I was a fucked-up person, and I was going to pay for all my wrong doing. All I was thinking about at this point was my wife. How the fuck did I let my life spiral out of control like this. I just sat back in the chair and waited for the cops to pick me up. I wasn't made for jail, so I wasn't even sure if I would last.

Terry

I had all the money and I was ready to go. I had to pack all my shit that I was taking with me and some of JJ's things. Jesse had agreed on letting me keep him for a couple of days. Of course, I had to kiss his ass and beg a little bit. He didn't know my ass wasn't planning on coming back. I stood for a second thinking of how fucking dumb Sharp's ass was. He swore I was going to call him once I got in the clear. Yeah ok…my ass was about to be out. Shit, hopefully Tyrell was on his way to beat his fat ass since I sent a video of Sarai sucking his little pecker.

I laughed at my handy work and headed back into my room. A loud bang at my door made me nearly jump out of my skin. When I got to the front door, I peeped out the window to see who it was and noticed it was Sarai. The tears in her eyes showed me that Tyrell must have found my little video. As soon as I opened the door, Sarai charged at me 'causing me to lose my footing, and she jumped right on top of me.

"You fucking stupid bitch. What have I done to you? For you to try and mess my happy life up." I didn't say anything. I just laughed at her simple ass.

"I hate you, bitch; it's just that simple. I hate that you're pretty, I hate that you're smart, I hate that Sharp wanted you instead of me. When I was fucking him and all you were doing was giving him weak ass head, I watched how you've been through so much, but you still standing. Then you end up with a rich fine ass nigga. I hate everything about you bitch."

I snapped while hitting her right in the face. Next thing I know we were sending punch after punch to each other. We were both born and raised in the hood, so we got down with the best of them. Sarai was starting to get the best of me when she was able to stand up and kick me right in my stomach.

"You sound so fucking stupid. If you wanted to be like me all you had to do was work on it. The rate you were going bitch you couldn't try to be me if I let you. Jealous cause Sharp wanted me. Hunny, I didn't want that stinking ass, fat mutha fucka, and I hope he gets fucked up the ass when he makes his way to the prison." Sarai said while sending another kick to my face this time.

She was about to kick me again until her little ass got lifted up and moved away from me. I tried to look up to see who it was, but my eye was swole shut already from being kicked in the face.

"Baby…what are you doing here? I told you to stay home while I handled this. How did you know she was the one that sent the video?" Tyrell asked.

"It would have made sense if her stupid ass would have used somebody else's phone. I have the number. You may not but I do. I guess she figured you were just going to go off on me. Her little-plan backfired. Now her stupid ass needs to go to jail with Sharp. I heard they both were blackmailing young girls to do sexual acts with them both."

"You a nasty, nasty bitch." The dude that was with them chuckled.

"She can go to jail right after her ass gives me my fucking money. Her and Sharp had a little plan, but the shit backfired, and Sharp's fat ass snitched. So, now he is on his way to jail. Where the fuck is my money ma? You got two minutes to answer or I'ma kill ya stupid ass."

"Please don't hurt me; it's all in my room in a duffle bag. I'm sorry. I didn't mean for all this to happen."

"Bitch, you ain't sorry so stop ya lying. That shit ain't gone get you out of this. You fucked with the wrong ones."

"What the fuck is going on in here." I heard Jesse's voice coming in the door.

"Yo, Jesse what's good my boy?" Tyrell asked.

"I'm good, bro; long time no see," Jesse said. I couldn't believe these niggas was having a whole conversation while I was on the floor.

"You know this chick?" Tyrell asked.

"Unfortunately, I do; it's my son's mother."

"Oh damn…I didn't know, bro. I thought JJ was you and Faith's son."

"Nah, I fucked up a while back, but what's going on?" He finally asked.

"Your baby mama…got herself into some shit. She was trying to rob me, and she and the fat mutha fucka at work had a whole sex scandal going on at the job. So, I'm about to call the cops on her dumb ass. I just came here to get my money she was trying to skip town with."

"Wait, so you were trying to leave town? Is that why you were trying to come to get JJ. Bitch, you were trying to leave with my son." Jesse snapped.

"This little bitch got a whole bunch of shit going on. Ma, you just be doing too damn much. Fucking fat, White men, helping him practically rape people, kidnapping, and robbery. You need to be underneath the fucking jail."

"Yo, Cam you here too?" Jesse said speaking to the other dude.

"What's good Jess?" The dude Cam spoke. "I got your money, bro. Come on; let's go before Keonna start calling me. I've been gone long enough; the closer it gets for her to have this baby she wanna be all up under me."

"I'm ready to go anyway. The cops on they way Jesse. I'm sorry this all went down my boy."

"Y'all good; she brought that shit on herself. She always trying to play tough, and her ass done took shit too far this time. Jail time may be what she needs to better herself."

This stupid ass had the nerve to be sitting there talking shit like he a good ass person. I couldn't. believe this. I just laid on the floor in tears waiting for the cops to come to take my ass to jail.

Chapter Twelve

Sarai

New Year's Eve....

It had been exactly five days since I thought my life was going to end. The day Tyrell got that video he woke me up out of my sleep going off. I thought he was about to kill my ass, but I finally explained to him what happened, and he watched the video over and noticed I was crying. He was mad that I didn't come to him about it. He said from the beginning I should have told him everything. I apologized, and he accepted it. The past few months have been every bit of amazing, and I couldn't imagine not spending the rest of my life with him.

"Baby, are you ready?" Tyrell asked while entering the bedroom. He stood peering at me like he was amazed at my appearance.

"Why are you staring at me like that?"

"You look amazing ma."

We were headed out to the big New Year's Ball that Tyrell and some of his colleagues throw every year. When he asked me to go, I said I didn't have anything to wear, and he laughed at me. The next day we went out and got me the most beautiful Vera Wang red strapless ballroom gown. I had my box braids up in a beautiful bun exposing my nice face beat. On my feet were a pair of simple gold red bottom pumps. Tyrell was matching my fly in an all-black Tom Ford suit with a red button-down shirt. A pair of Gucci

Donnie Web leather loafers adorned his feet. His dreads were neatly placed in a french braid. He was staring at me like he wanted to strip me out of my clothes. What little did he know I was feeling the same way.

"Thank you, baby. Now, let's get out of here before we end up not going anywhere." Once we made it to the living room Ms. Joyce and my mama were sitting on the couch.

"Oh my God…you two look so great." My mama beamed with a smile on her face. She had been staying with us. She said she was serious about getting help, so Tyrell insisted she stay with us then after the holidays we send her to a program. She was down with it and I was so happy.

"Yes…they do. You two look amazing. Go on out and have you a good time son." Ms. Joyce cooed.

Her and my mama had become so close and they help so much with the kids. I had been the acting store manager at the store until Tyrell found someone that was qualified. I mean, I was, but he didn't want me working at that store anymore. So, when he found one, I would be going to another store. At first, he said he didn't want me to work anymore, but I wasn't off that. Shit, we just started out, now if we ever get married then I'll consider being a stay home mama. I assured him that I still wanted to do something. Sitting home had not been a norm for me since Trey passed. How all that went down, it made me learn that I should always have my own.

"Thanks, mama, and don't wait up." Tyrell beamed.

Once we made it out the door a car pulled up on the side of us. Then a driver got out and opened the door for us.

"I didn't know you hired a driver baby."

"Yeah, I wanted both of us to drink, party, and enjoy ourselves."

I got in the car and Tyrell climbed in right behind me. The party was at this place called The Mansion in Voorhees. I heard of it before, but I have never been inside. I knew of it being one of those expensive venues. I remember a basketball player got married there. I think it was Allen Iverson.

"Oh ok…I'm with that." I smiled while looking out of the window.

"Sarai, do you ever want more kids?" Tyrell asked shocking the hell out of me.

"Yes…I've always wanted a lot. I guess cause my mama only had me. What about you?"

"Yeah… me too. I've always said I wanted about five."

"Five is not too many. I really never put a limit on how many I wanted. I just know I wanted a lot. I just wanted to be married and be able to take care of them without struggling. My mama would always say I needed a rich husband for all the kids I wanted."

"Your mama is so funny. I'm really enjoying her staying with us. Do you think she's ready for the help?" Tyrell asked.

"Yeah, I think she's ready. If she wasn't, she would have been dipped off."

The car came to a stop. So, I assumed that we were at the venue already. The driver hopped out and opened the door for us. Tyrell got out then helped me out. The place was beautifully decorated. Everyone that was getting out was looking like celebrities. I didn't know it was like this in the corporate world, but then again, all money makers party together.

"You ready to go in baby?"

"I guess…it's just that I've never been around all of this."

"You'll be fine; just follow my lead," Tyrell assured me while grabbing my hand.

When we walked in, it was every bit of amazing; the music was playing and everyone was mingling. I was so nervous I grabbed the first drink I saw. The ladies were walking around with drinks on trays. A couple of people were coming our way, and Tyrell grabbed my hand.

"Sarai, this is Mr. and Mrs. Collins, Mr. Collins was my father's boss for many years. He was the one that mentored my father when it was time for him to own one of his very own stores. He even showed me the ropes when my father passed."

"Hello, Tyrell and Ms. Sarai. It's nice to meet you, young lady. Tyrell, how is your mother doing?"

"She is doing fine; she sends her love."

"Hunny, you're wearing that dress." Ms. Collins complimented me.

"Why you think Tyrell picked it out? He said I had to have it. He needed to see me in it."

"Well, he did good my dear. Come with me, and let's go have girl talk, while the fellas talk business." Ms. Collins insisted.

I didn't even know what to say. I didn't know this woman, but I had to get used to this. I knew in the future I would have more events like this to attend. This was new to me. I was used to the street type niggas. Hell, Trey and I was together for a minute, and this was far from a house party.

"I know you're not used to this, but these events can be fun." Ms. Collins pleaded.

"Do I look that obvious?" I asked in a low tone.

"Yes…but it's ok. I remember being just like you when Mark first brought me to one of these things. Believe it or not some of these stuck-up people do know how to party. Don't let the looks fool you. Shit, I was born and raised in Camden, New Jersey myself. I just know how to turn it on and off. When I wanna act a fool I will, and when I wanna be stuck up I will." She giggled causing me to smile.

"I'm from Camden, New Jersey, too. I was raised out East Camden."

"Oh ok… how long have you been dating Tyrell? I've never seen him so happy before. I can also tell from the way he looks at you that he is madly in love."

"I met him right before Thanksgiving at one of his stores."

"Mmm…and he got you at this event already. Yeah, he feeling you. How do you feel about him?" At first, I felt like she was being a little nosey with this question but then again, I liked her conversation.

"I love him, but a little scared since it's so soon. Some days, I be feeling like we moving too fast then others I'm like I want all of this man."

"If he asks you to marry him will you say yes?"

"I wanna see him in my future, so yeah I probably would."

"Well, that means you've found your true love. Let it flow baby. You answered that question with no hesitation and that says a lot. Just follow your heart baby girl; it will never steer you wrong. Now go enjoy your man, and when he pops that question make sure you remind him to send me an invite." Ms. Collins said while walking away. I felt Tyrell rap his arms around my waist.

"You good?" He asked while kissing my neck.

"Yes…I'm great now that you're here."

"Special request from Mr. McKnight himself." The DJ yelled through the microphone.

"Come on, let's dance," Tyrell asked while grabbing my hand and pulling me to the dance floor.

Fall For You By. *Leela James* blared through the speakers. This was one of my favorite songs. I didn't even know Tyrell knew that.

Here we are together

And everything between us is good

I'm right here in this cloud, baby

Ready to fly but before I take another step, would you catch me if I fall for you?

Tyrell and I danced like we were the only ones in the room. I swear tonight felt like some movie type shit, but I didn't want any of it to end. I was enjoying myself with the new love of my life. After the song ended, we kissed each other right in the middle of the floor.

"Alright everyone, it's almost that time. Do anyone want the mic to tell us their last wishes of 2018." The DJ asked. Tyrell grabbed my hand and dragged me up on the stage with him.

"Twenty eighteen has been a trying year for me with my businesses and things that were going on in my life, but near the end, I think I found my soulmate. Sarai, you and your kids came in my life and showed me that it's possible to love in a short time. For that, I don't wanna come into 2019 without us taking what we have to the next level." Tyrell then got down on one knee, and I almost lost it. Was this man about to ask me to marry him in just three months' time?

"Tyrell, what you doing down there baby? Get up." I said just above a whisper.

"Sarai, will you marry me, baby?" He asked while opening this red box. When I looked in the box and saw the ring I almost fainted. I had to think in my head for a couple of minutes before I answered. Being engaged didn't mean we were getting married tomorrow, and I did say I wanted to spend the rest of my life with this man.

"Yess, Tyrell, I will marry you. Yess baby." I said as tears fell from my face. The minute I said yes, the countdown began. "10,9,8,7,6,5,4,3,2 ,1 HAPPY NEW YEAR'S!"

Tyrell and I ended 2018 with a bang. I went from having a rough time to entering a new year with a new man that loved me and my kids. We needed him, and he needed us, and now it's time for us to begin our new journey in the new year…

The End...